To
Ron & Irene
Rappert.
Best wishes

Sharon P. Clapp

The Pringle Progression

smaller/fewer

a novel by Sheldon Wimpfen

*A solution to the world's
most defining problem?*

American Literary Press, Inc.
Five Star Special Edition
Baltimore, Maryland

The Pringle Progression

Library of Congress
Cataloging in Publication Data
ISBN 1-56167-413-3

Library of Congress Card Catalog Number:
97-078335

Published by

American Literary Press, Inc.
Five Star Special Edition
8019 Belair Road, Suite 10
Baltimore, Maryland 21236

Manufactured in the United States of America

CHAPTER 1
TROUBLE ON PLANET EARTH

Juana Terranova paused in her task of picking coca leaves high on the east slope of the Andes. Juana was fourteen and had been a coca picker for six years to help her family survive in the laggard Colombian economy. Picking coca was hard work as one had to bend over constantly to find and pull the near-round leaves from the low-growing coca bushes. Juana wore a vari-colored skirt woven of alpaca fur, an off-white loose blouse and a somewhat tattered straw hat to ward off the merciless heat of the sun. Her feet were shod with the ubiquitous 6.50x16s, sandals made from old tire casings. A home-made knife in a leather sheath flopped loosely from a thong around her waist.

It was a lonely job as the pickers were scattered over a long mountainside. The slopes where the low cocoa bushes flourished stretched off to the peaks of the Andes and their cloud-capped crowns. Although the task was a solitary one, there was always joy and inspiration in viewing the awesome mountain scenery that seemed to go on forever to vanishing horizons. Juana drug the large coca sack behind her. Now nearly half full, its growing weight was almost too much for her as the heat of the day increased. Suddenly Juana yelped in pain. "Por Dios! Que paso?"

Juana had cramps that were growing in frequency and intensity. At the risk of being yelled at and perhaps struck by the field supervisor, Juana moved to the sparse shade of a Eucalyptus tree and rested hoping the pains would cease. Instead the pains increased as she felt the wet flood when her water broke.

Perspiration rolled off her face. She looked up and saw a condor floating lazily in the cerulean sky. Juana thought for a few moments that she would be the next meal for the huge carnivore. Painful spasms wracked her small body. She grasped the tree trunk and screamed. There was no one near enough to hear. Soon she was overcome and gave birth to a rather tiny baby.

Small as she was, not over five feet, Juana was shocked to see the tiny three or four pound child. Juana tied off the umbilical cord with some threads from her skirt and cut it before swaddling the babe in a piece of her blouse.

The tiny baby was the outcome of a torrid liaison with a neighbor boy but a few years older than she. Juana had no idea that she was pregnant until the few minutes before the baby's arrival.

Juana had an attraction for young men and they were drawn to her. She was well formed with a slender waist, a nice wiggle to her stern with a matching wobble to her firm but ample breasts. Her dark brown eyes had a mischievous glint and her bright smile hinted of warm pleasures when she chatted with the male coca pickers. In months past she had intrigued a young coca picker. He wasted no time in putting Juana down on the ground between the rows of coca plants, lifting her many skirts and pinning her down while he penetrated her with near frantic action. Juana thought he was great fun. The excitement he generated was enjoyable and she made sure that their mutual pleasure was repeated for the next several days

Jose Cruz, a sixteen year old coca picker, watched from a distance as Juana gave birth. He knew exactly what was happening as he had already fathered two other, but larger babies. But Jose wasn't sure he was the father of this one as he knew that Juana had indulged in sexual sessions with a number of the other male coca pickers.

Jose did know that he was the first to pluck the pleasure of Juana's hairless smooth pubic mound. After all, there

2   Wimpfen

wasn't a great deal to do in the remote coca-growing area and sex with a variety of lovers was fun to Juana.

Juana rested while she raised her blouse and placed a small brown nipple in the mouth of her newborn son. He suckled greedily.

It was now close to the end of the shift and the field supervisor came by leading four llamas. Some were already loaded with sacks of the day's pick of coca. He laughed when he saw Juana with her babe at breast. "This had to happen. It happens to all of you girls. I just didn't know when as you didn't swell like the others."

He picked up her sack and weighed it on a small beam scale. "Kind of light today. You're going to have to pick faster now that you have another mouth to feed."

Juana ignored him. She rose to her feet with the tiny baby in her arms and walked down the path to a small village of stone huts that huddled at the base of the mountain. There were a few dozen one-room stone shacks in the village and Juana walked to one close to the edge of the group, raised the flap that served as a door and entered. Her mother took note of the the new child at a glance saying, "That's what comes from fooling around."

The same thing had happened to her two older daughters, so the newborn baby came as no surprise. Juana's mother peeked into the bundle she held and exclaimed, "What a tiny one? I wonder if it will survive?"

Small wonder that the population of Columbia was predicted to double in 34 years. It was the year 2000 A.D.

Far to the north, in Juneau, Alaska, eighteen-year old Joan Cummings enjoyed her life style. She skied on the Juneau ice cap whenever the opportunity arose. She fished for salmon and hiked with friends from her high school class. Joan was popular with both her girl friends and her boy friends. Her ever-ready smile, bright blue eyes over a pert nose and blond hair that streamed behind her as she skied enhanced her attractiveness. At 116 pounds, her five foot five inch frame was well muscled and well proportioned. She didn't lack for dates, but was drawn particularly to a high school classmate, Dan Munson.

During the summer, both Joan and Dan worked at the salmon bake held daily in the area of the old mine shops of the now defunct Alaska Juneau mine. Each day they drove together up Gold Creek gorge above the town to the old Gold Creek Tunnel and worked at preparing the salmon bake for the horde of hungry tourists that would begin to arrive about 5 PM. Many came up the narrow twisting road from Juneau while others hiked down the trail from the Perseverance Basin.

Dan stood six foot two in his bare feet and weighed a lean 200 pounds. His tawny skin, aquiline nose and deep-set black eyes did more than hint of Dan's mixed ancestry of Tlingit and Russian. Dan had an engaging and ready smile and the tourists liked to have Dan serve their slabs of roasted salmon.

Weekends Dan worked with his father on his salmon fishing boat. Dan's ambition was to own a similar vessel and spend his days as a commercial salmon fisherman. Dan and Joan spent much of their free time together. They particularly enjoyed taking the Munson boat out for a day of fishing on their own. They fished in fair weather and foul.

They were always prepared to sleep on the boat but never had to until one day they were caught by a sudden storm near Elfin Cove. There was nothing they could do about getting back to Juneau so they agreed to make the best of the situation. Grilled salmon steaks and canned vegetables were prepared by Joan while Dan's rummaging turned up a bottle of Leibfraumilch his dad had been hoarding.

Warmed by the good meal and the wine, the setting was conducive to what was to be expected. Their flaming hormones drew them together. Their short courtship culminated in a marriage without delay soon after their night on the boat when Joan realized that she was carrying their child.

Everything seemed normal except that Joan's belly just didn't seem to swell to the size she had anticipated.

After a normal term, Joan gave birth to a perfectly formed but tiny infant surprising herself, the father and the child's grandparents. This anomalous appearance of less-than-normal sized babies was being repeated around the world. Obstetricians were amazed, but had no clue as to what was happening.

"All the babies are smaller!" exclaimed Nancy Dearborn, head nurse in the obstetric section of Denver General Hospital. For months Nancy had suspected something strange was going on and finally the idea became clear. The babies were smaller and consistently so. Nancy's conclusion needed confirmation. She made phone calls to several of her peers elsewhere.

"Hello, Juanita. This is Nancy Dearborn in Denver. Haven't talked to you in a century. How have you been?"

"Why I'm fine, Nancy. Am sure glad you called. I've been thinking about you lots lately. I was about to get around to calling you," said Juanita

"What I'm calling about is something strange that appears to be happening here. It seems that all the babies being born here are getting smaller. Even though their mothers have carried them for full term, it's almost as if they were preemies when you look at the size of them. I just wonder if it's a situation unique to here or if you have noticed anything."

"Nancy, I'm bothered about the same thing but was reluctant to talk about it for fear folks would think I was nuts. But almost all of our babies are below average size. And we haven't a clue as to why. They all seem healthy and normal except for being small. Our average baby seems to be running less than four pounds. A year ago the average was about seven or eight pounds. What do you think is happening?"

Nancy's calls to other nurses that were in her graduating class resulted in similar conversations. Something profound and shattering was taking place, but none knew how or why. The portent of the proliferation of under-sized babies was awesome!

The sun was midway in its morning path. The air was clear but thin at the 11, 992 ft. elevation of the summit of Loveland Pass. Fleecy white clouds walked in procession towards the east. Not far below was the tree line where Engelman spruce danced in the wind. The quaking Aspen moved, shaking their golden leaves.They quivered in waves as errant breezes stirred their limbs.

There was not a vehicle in sight as the old road across the pass was seldom used since the completion of the Eisenhower tunnel. Only four-wheel drive cars could navigate the now near impassable road. This made no difference to Steve Pringle as he had followed the old road on foot.

After overnighting at Dillon, Steve had driven east to the point where the old road to Loveland Pass took off. and parked his Jeep. Then he shouldered his pack and headed east towards Denver. The old road was easy to follow and, as he moved steadily upwards, Steve found the solitude and brisk breeze much to his liking.

Here, in late September, the snow banks were still retreating in the mid-day sun, but were ready to accept the snowfalls that could come at any time as fall advanced. Here, on the Continental Divide, the views in every direction were spectacular. Rough ridges and rugged snow-crowned peaks filled the scenes to the north and south and west. The range dropped off to the east as far away the great plains might be seen were it not for the faint haze that obscured Steve's vision. Steve was filled with a feeling of exhilaration but had no one to share it with.

Sixty miles to the east lay Denver. Steve took off his pack and looked for a soft rock on which to rest. He munched on a handful of raisins from the side pocket of his pack, his back against the old sign that marked the summit of Loveland Pass. He knew that, by this time of morning, Denver already lay under a pall of brownish nitrous oxides that accumulated each day as the traffic increased. It wasn't pleasant to think what growth had done to Denver.

For years Denver's population was virtually stalled for lack of water. But then, when the maxim that water could only be used in the valley of its origin was changed, western slope water was diverted through tunnels under the Continental Divide. Denver's population zoomed. Half a century ago doctors urged their pulmonary patients to move to Denver where the air was fresh and clean. Not so today.

The press of Denvers growing population and its numerous autos had changed Denver's atmosphere to something less than desirable. But Denver was far from unique. Back in 1978, not quite a quarter of a century past, the world's population was 4.2 billion. Now in the year 2000, it was estimated that the world hosted some 5.8 billion people with a forecasted 7 billion by 2010 and 8.4 billion in the year 2025. The automobile population, at least in the United States, had grown proportionately.

Steve Pringle was born and raised in Idaho Springs. His dad and his granddad had worked nearby all their lives. Sometimes they worked in one or the other of the operating mines in the area and sometimes they looked for a complex of rocks and minerals that might become a mine. Both of Steve's male predecessors had dreamed of finding and operating a mine of their own. That dream was never realized, but neither did they ever give up.

At times they worked on one payroll or another, but they applied themselves more industriously when they were off in the mountains digging and panning. Now and then they came across concentrations of minerals that warranted the staking of claims. This they did in various county courthouses.

The claims were worked and hopes soared but, with appalling frequency, these hopes were dashed as their discoveries failed to amount to something of economic importance. Nearly a half century had passed since Steve's grandfather had found and operated a successful uranium mine southeast of Moab, Utah. There the senior Pringle had mined and shipped to the Moab buying station of the Atomic Energy Commission thousands of tons of rich uraninite ore that averaged more than one-half percent uranium. That single success had enriched the eldest Pringle and left him with a chronic compulsion to find still another bonanza.

Steve was born in the modest home his grandfather had built from logs cut in the nearby mountains and hauled to town. As a child he was frequently taken on trips to the mountains to watch with a growing curiosity as the elder Pringles picked at rocks, dug and panned. His quick mind unconsciouly absorbed knowledge of rocks and minerals and how they occurred. At the same time he grasped the geology of the places visited.

Steve attended high school in Idaho Springs where, in addition to the studies that were taken by all, he played football and became a star on the school's ski team. Steve dated a few girls now and then but those rare events took a back seat to his sports, prospecting, and hunting and fishing with his dad. Steve's mother Marie, Colorado born, made a real home for her family, Steve, his dad and his younger sister, Anne. Anne looked up to her three-year-older brother as her hero and protector. She was always ready to join Steve and her dad, and, frequently, mother Marie, to enjoy the Colorado Front Range and the unlimited opportunities to find new vistas and fishing holes.

It was a foregone conclusion that Steve would attend the nearby Colorado School of Mines at Golden. Steve was raised on table talk about his forthcoming career in mining and he never gave a thought to any alternative. He saw mining as a real challenge and was entranced by the idea of seeing something no one had ever seen before as each drill round blasted revealed a fresh rock face, hopefully with signs of mineralization.

"Steve," his grandfather said, "One of the greatest thrills in the world is to make a good discovery. When the demand for uranium was high back in the early 50s, I headed for Grand Junction to find out what it was all about. The day I went out to visit the AEC compound right at the junction of the Colorado and the Gunnison rivers, I found out that there were about 60 other fellows with the very same idea as mine. But them fellers in the AEC knew what they were doing. They had all sorts of reading material that they handed out and we could each have a session with one of the AEC mining engineers or geologists. The fellow that talked to me said there were several good ways to about finding a likely prospect. One was to look for your elephant where other elephants had been found and the other was to go into virgin country that hadn't been explored.

"There was this guy Charlie Steen that made a fabulous find rich in pitchblende in Big Indian Wash, so that's where I decided to hunt my elephant.

"A lot of careful thought had gone into the planning of the program. They knew that there would be lots of headaches and wheel spinning if the job was carried out with government employees. So a system was designed to get the most possible participation of private miners and mining companies.

"The AEC mapped the country with their own people and contractors. All the geologic data was available to anyone. Should a miner come across some uranium ore there was an area market for it at one or the other of the buying stations they built. You could deliver a truck load of ore and get paid for it in a few hours. That time was necessary to weigh, sample and assay the ore.

"Believe me, that was a great program and when I operated my claims down in Big Indian Wash, I produced a lot of good ore and made more money in two years than I ever did before or since.

"The odds are pretty good that you can be a successful miner if you work hard and examine enough prospects. The records show that about one in a thousand prospects becomes a mine. So get with it Steve and you might just find that one good prospect."

"Gee, grandpa! I never heard you talk so long about your uranium find before. What got into you?"

"Well, sometimes I wonder if you really will go on and get your degree and go into the mining business. So, I felt like you needed a bit of encouragement."

"It just never occurred to me to do anything else. All my life has been, in some way, connected with mines and mineral and mining is what I want to do. Compared to anything else I've got a leg up in that field."

"Sure wish I could take that computer with me. It would be a real help in doing my school work."

"I was hoping you would take it," chimed in Anne. "Then we could get a newer one for the family. Besides that thing is four years old, or at least three generations in computer lives."

Grandpa Pringle smiled saying, "I've got a surprise for you, Steve, and this is about as good a time to spring it on you as any. Just sit tight and close your eyes." Going to a large walk in closet, the old man pulled out a number of huge boxes that looked like they were covered with cow hide. "OK, Steve, you can open up now."

Steve immediately recognized the containers. "Wow, thanks grandpa. That is just what I need to make things easier at Mines." He couldn't wait to open it up. "This is the latest thing out. It has recordable CD-ROM and the fastest processor available. I'll be the envy of all the guys in my class. Am glad it has a lock so I can keep others from getting into it. Thanks again grandpa."

So Steve attended Mines. It wasn't that far from Idaho Springs to Golden, so Steve decided to commute in his old GMC pickup. That didn't last long as he became so involved that he needed more time on campus and moved in to one of the dorms.

His freshman year included courses on geology, mineralogy, chemistry, algebra, surveying and physics. He studied long and hard and there wasn't much time for extracurricular activities. He made good grades and earned the reputation with his profs as being consistently dependable. The first summer at Mines he spent with his class at the school's experimental mine near Idaho Springs.

He liked this as he spent the evening at home with his family. In his sophomore year he studied hard and played hard. In addition to being on the football team Steve participated in many school activities, from painting the M high on Lookout Mountain to squiring the girls that came to Golden to enjoy the college dances.

Summer vacation times were spent in working as a mucker, miner, trackman or timberman in one or the other of the nearby small mines. Steve graduated with honors and looked forward to a career in mining in strange lands in another part of the world.

At 27, Steve was depressed. Six years of a near idyllic marriage to Susan was now history. They had met at one of the dances at Mines and seemed to be attracted to each other immediately.The tall willowy blonde with breasts like ripe melons attracted Steve like a powerful magnet.

"Golly your a good dancer. You're so light on your feet that I feel like I'm dancing with a feather-a fullsome one that is."

"Thanks a lot. I like dancing with you too. You move with grace and you don't hold me too tight."

They shared many dances that evening and made plans to see each other again. "How about taking a weekend ride with me? My folks live in Idaho Springs and I try to get there every weekend that I can. It would be fun if you could come with me this Saturday and meet my family. I think you would like them and I know they would enjoy your company. How about it Sue?"

"Hmm, let me see. I do have this weekend free and a visit to Idaho Springs would be fun. I'd like to meet your family too. Will there be a chance to do a bit of fishing?"

"Sure, bring your rod and tackle and we can try Clear Creek. There are some fine rainbows in Clear Creek and I've caught a few 18 inchers. I'll call mom and get things set up. I'm sure she would want us to stay long enough to have lunch with them and then we can fish as we head home via the Clear Creek road."

Saturday was bright and clear. Steve drove to Denver to pick up Sue and they headed to Idaho Springs in Steve's rather beat-up GMC pickup. The Pringles welcomed Sue and she seemed to fit in well. The Pringles liked Sue and were pleased that she was so open and responsive to their many questions. Marie had fixed a light lunch after which Steve and Sue said their goodbyes.

"Sue, it was great having you for a few hours. You're welcome any time and we do want to see you again and soon." commented Marie.

Heading down the road via Clear Creek, Steve parked the pickup on a spoil bank from one of the tunnels. They both rigged their ultra-light rods eagerly as they prepared to clamber down the bank and try to catch a few trout.

The sun was still high, perhaps not the best time to catch fish. But the pair worked their way up the stream bank and cast repeatedly in likely looking water.

"Hey! I've got one on. I think he's a pretty good sized one the way he's fighting." Just then the trout broke water leaping nearly a foot above the water as it shook the lure from its jaw. "Aw hell! "was all that Sue could say as her quarry gave a flash and vanished.

Both Steve and Sue persisted and before the sun dropped behind the Front Range they each had a pair of fine rainbows that would make an ample meal. Tired but happy, they walked back to the pickup.

"Gee, that was a wonderful day. I feel so glad to be alive to enjoy such a day. Your family was just grand and already I feel close to them.Then the fishing. I'm exhausted but oh so happy. Take me home and I'll cook you up a huge trout dinner with all the fixings."

Sue did herself proud in the kitchen. During the meal Steve remembered his Mother saying now and then, 'Don't mess around with any woman who isn't good in the kitchen for she probably won't be any good in the other rooms either!'" They both enjoyed a big laugh when Steve told this family story.

Their friendship blossomed. They spent as much time as possible together even though the press of school activities was a full schedule by itself. Before the year ran out they were wed at a tasteful ceremony in Golden. Sue's parents flew in for the event.

Susan continued at Denver University while Steve pursued his studies for his final year at Golden. Steve had hoped to go abroad to start his mining career but that idea fell apart as Sue had begun her career in commercial art in downtown Denver. And she wasn't about to give that up for a lonesome life in some African nation or in the high Andes of South America. As a product of eastern Pennsylvania, life in a remote wilderness had little appeal.

"I just can't do it, Steve. Ever since I was a kid scratching stuff on scraps of paper, I've wanted to break into the art field in one way or another. It is just too much to ask me to throw away all my years of training to be a housewife in some remote place in Australia."

Steve had been offered a lucrative job at a huge open pit iron mine in northwestern Australia and was itching to go. But Susan was precious to him and he felt that he had to compromise somehow.

So he found his first job as a mining engineer in the Henderson molybdenum mine just west of Empire in the shadow of Red Mountain. Berthoud Pass was a bit beyond the road to the mine.

This mine had always fascinated Steve. He was aware of how it was discovered by the expertise of Stewart Wallace and the perseverance of Robert Henderson is pursuing depositional concepts deduced from the overlying Urad orebody.

It was a challenge to Steve to conduct the further development and production from the Henderson Mine from its more than 50 miles of underground openings. Each day he looked forward to performing his work in such a manner as to maximize mine output and, at the same time, adhere faithfully to the precepts of care and respect for this remarkable national asset.

Steve and Susan acquired a home in Evergreen a community that gave them both an acceptable commute. Their life together was enjoyable and satisfying. They managed to work out vacation times together and traveled to Yellowstone, Yosemite, Glacier and other National parks. Weekends together fishing and hiking in the summer and skiing in the winter fulfilled both Sue and Steve.

Steve spent most of each shift underground. He laid out the survey lines for the development headings and set the location of scram drifts and draw chutes for the huge block caving mine. Then for several hours each day he was involved in planning the development of additional ore blocks for future extraction. It was a satisfying job and Steve was keenly aware of how his planning affected total output of molybdenum ore and concentrates of a quality and quantity that had a pronounced bearing on the companies balance sheet.

Steve and Sue both loved the mountains and the many secret and quiet places encouraged their search for a weekend home site where they could retreat from the hustle and bustle of everyday life. They hiked up long valleys and over passes to look at spots that might fill their desires. Either the place didn't suit their dreams or the price was too high. But they kept on looking for the place to have a second home.

When Steve learned that the five patented claims of the long defunct Minnesota Mines, about five miles north of

Empire, were to be sold at auction he had to have another look.

"Honey, I think I've found what we're looking for. When I was going to school, I worked at this mine one summer. It's a great place, snug in a high valley that faces to the south. And there's a flat area formed by the old mine waste dumps. Let's go have a look!"

"Sounds good to me. We've looked at so many places and nothing seemed quite right. With you knowing this spot, perhaps this could be what we want. Let's go!"

The next Saturday they drove up to Empire. Steve knew the country well. They passed Idaho Springs when Steve commented. "This is where the old Red Elephant mine was. There used to be a trestle over the old dirt road. That trestle carried the hand-trammed ore from that portal you can barely see. The mill building had a great big red elephant painted on the wall."

At Empire they left the main road and turned right up the badly eroded road that led to the old Minnesota Mines mill site. The mill building was crumbling as was the old assay office and change house. All equipment had long since been removed. Even the narrow gauge track that led from the mine portal to the still-standing Gilpin County sorting bin had been removed. The site appealed to both as they looked over the near flat area and south to spectacular mountain scenes.

"I just remembered something. Back in the mid thirties, my granddad worked in this area. I recall his mentioning Empire and a gold mine and particularly a Gilpin County sorting bin that he helped build. Grandpa said that the mine didn't have much good grade ore, but he felt that if its development ever got to the right place for deposition temperatures and pressures, there was a good chance that there could be a zone in the vein where free gold would be found. Unfortunately that spot was never found."

"I don't care if this place never produces any gold!" exclaimed Susan. "I just love this spot and think we should make a high enough bid to be damn sure that we get it. Now that we've found a place we both like, I just couldn't stand it if we lost it to another bidder."

There were few bidders at the auction. Perhaps the awesome rutted access road kept them away. To their pleasant surprise, Steve and Susan learned their bid was the highest and they were now owners of 100 acres of rough land at the end of the twisting five mile road north from Empire. The property was covered with Engelman spruce and lodge pole pine. The upper end was close to timberline. Now their dream of a summer cabin retreat could be fulfilled.

They kept on with their normal daily lives. In the long winter evenings they made plans for their cabin in the mountains. They skied on the weekends and looked forward to the joy they found in hiking and fishing in the warmer months.

But it couldn't last! Sues competence caught the eye of an executive from a New York City firm who made Sue an offer she couldn't refuse. Reluctantly, Sue packed her bags to move to the big city. Their parting was tearful, but they reassured each other that they would be together frequently. Their time together soon degenerated to hasty weekends in Denver, Chicago and New York. They had fun but soon the weekends were further and further apart. Separation and divorce by mutual consent soon followed as the long distance existence satisfied neither. In the property settlement Susan took the bank accounts and other liquid assets. Steve got their home in Evergreen and the cabin north of Empire. There were no children to complicate the procedure and they remained good friends.

The home held many memories and, at times, Steve was overwhelmed with the sadness of what had gone wrong in their lives. He was restless and spent much of his off time with friends hiking and fishing. Now and then he dated some Denver girl for dinner, dancing and whatever. A few even went camping and fishing with him but none of them measured up. Anyhow, Steve just wasn't ready for another commitment. His strong appetite for sex was satisfied where he found it. But when the enjoyment of a female companion began to pall, Steve ended the relationship and moved on.

Often he ate out alone or put together lonely meals at home. Frequently he would dine with his neighbors, Alan and Mary Muster. Alan was a geneticist and taught and did research at Denver University. The Musters had enjoyed their friendly and active neighbors and, although Sue was gone, they were happy to keep Steve as a trusted friend. Unlike Steve who was tall and slender for all his 180 pounds, Alan was a bit chubby at five foot six inches and 165 pounds.

Steve had a slightly aquiline nose. His firm chin, engaging smile, gray eyes and wavy brown hair were among the attributes that appealed to his feminine companions. His broad shoulders, slim hips and well-muscled limbs added to his charisma. His low, deep voice forever seemed to be imparting some confidence.

Alan, at 32, found that his blond hair was getting sparse. He had a small bald spot that seemed endearing to Mary who frequently caressed it with affection. What hair he had left often dangled in the way of the glasses Alan wore continuously.

Steve and Alan were close friends and shared many a campfire after they fished the streams of nearby mountain valleys. Now and then they would head for Glenwood Springs and fish the Roaring Fork, the Marble and other streams on the western slope. When time permitted they would travel further west to the lakes of Grand Mesa. Steve kept an old four-wheel drive Jeep station wagon that was always ready to go. His and Alan's camping gear were

18

stowed in the Jeep to cut down on delays in getting ready for a wilderness venture.

Like all ardent trout fisherman, they found that the quality of the fishing increased as the square of the distance they had to hike from the place they left the car. They hiked in to many lakes on Grand Mesa, with Never Sweat being one of their favorites. It was a four mile uphill hike to Never Sweat. There wasn't much air at 10,000 ft. and the long walk was a strain. They seldom ran into any competing fishermen at that remote lake. And the fishing was great. Although they released most of the trout that were lured to bite on their hand-tied flies, they always kept a few of the smaller ones and several two pounders for a good meal.

They played hard in the daylight hours and held serious discussions in the glow of the fading campfires that had cooked their evening meal of broiled trout. Both men shared concern over the direction the human race was taking. Large or small, both held positive opinions and were prone to make judgments about what was taking place in the United States and the rest of the world.

The disturbing period of the late 1900s was history and had been succeeded by an administration that had struggled and achieved a measure of recovery from the economic and social experiments that were popular in the past. What had been an ever burgeoning national debt appeared to be under control and even reduced. Various experiments with the armed forces had come close to impairing the military competence of the United States. But the road back to a degree of normalcy had finally taken hold and volunteers were again filling the ranks.

"I'm really bothered."said Steve."Those Balkan countries just won't give it up. They keep on squabbling and, worse yet, the many horrors of the Holocaust are being repeated now and then. But still, the world's populations grow and grow despite the lack of enough food to go around."

"Food isn't the only shortage. Even drinking water is getting scarce. Look at Turkey. It's Ataturk Dam reduced the supply to Iraq and now they're at war."

Great were the human losses in this and other wars that raged in different parts of the world. But these conflicts failed to have a lasting impact on the growth of populations.

"It seems to me," commented Alan, "That the returning warriors become more prolific and go out of their way to inseminate as many females as possible whether it be their own or those of the defeated nation."

"I'm bothered too as marriage seems to be out of favor more and more. The number of young people who set up light housekeeping is going up and so are the numbers of illegitimate kids. This impairment of the family structure results in too many kids with a poor foundation fostering still more crime and more bastards."

"There are other changes too." said Steve. "Years ago I visited Stockholm for a brief stay at the Grand Hotel. One evening some friends took me to dinner at an ancient inn on an island. The main entry was less than six feet high and we had to keep our heads down to get to a table."

Throughout the world nations blessed with an adequate diet found that succeeding generations were taller thereby making even greater impacts on the use of resources. Here in the United States there were still many homes where today's folk had to stoop to enter.How could that growth trend be reversed so that consumption of food and raw materials could be conserved?

Overpopulation, the defining crisis of the world, became the subject of Steve's and Alan's discussions time and again for it seemed to be the fulcrum on which all of the world's other problems balanced. Steve addressed the problem from the engineer's point of view. Billions of dollars for foreign aid and military assistance had been squandered on the underdeveloped countries of the world with but little impact on their major problem - population growth. And a large percentage of these people were hungry most of the time. Many were starving and the frequency and distribution of famines increased.

Our incursion into Somalia was history and subsequent events reflected continued growth of Somalia's population many of whom were doomed to starve. Somalia was far from unique as similar situations existed in the Sudan and India to name a few of those imperiled nations.

Steve snorted, "Hungry, hell, it seems like starvation is a constant threat if not a way of life or, more properly, a way of death. And it's going to get worse as populations increase. There sure isn't any increase in arable land and fertilizers.

"I remember a paper by Ira Joralemon, an eminent mining engineer, who addressed that problem. He wrote an article in 1963 called *Forever Hunger or What Price World Prosperity?* Ira explored world use of metals and minerals within three groups of countries. Group I included the USA, Canada, Western Europe, Australia and New Zealand. Group II consisted of Russia and its European Satellites, Siberia and Japan. He had a Group III that comprised Latin America, Africa, Asia and Indonesia, but not Japan. Ira explored the consumption of eight key metals by these groups as well as the fertilizer minerals, and energy consumption.

"He concluded that the parallelism between the relative per capita use of eight key materials and the average income per person was so striking that these commodities could be accepted as adequate indices of the economies of the backward countries. But to acquire the raw materials and manufactured goods that must precede freedom from hunger, they would have to increase their income by more than a thousand billion dollars a year. There isn't a ghost of a chance of getting that and the annual increases in population makes the problem worse.

"Why here in the United States man's consumption of raw materials on a per capita basis per year is staggering. Each one of us uses about 20 tons of resources. That includes such quantities as 4 tons of petroleum, 3 tons of coal, 2 tons of natural gas plus about 0.6 ton of iron and steel, 4 tons of stone, 60 pounds of aluminum and 13 pounds of lead plus lots of other stuff. We are rapidly depleting our resources and depending more and more on imports. And the rest of the world is also increasing its demands as it become more industrialized.."

Alan concurred and added, "It sure is a complex problem that's aggravated by the breakup of the family. Genes mean a lot and what is happening is that the least intelligent of the world's peoples are reproducing at the fastest rate. And that means that there will be fewer and fewer people with the intelligence to help solve the dilemma. Further it is the countries with the least ability to feed its people that are reproducing at the fastest rate. How can a world win when those with the most deficient genes are increasingly a higher percentage of the world's population?"

"Yep, the world has a real problem. It's people face mass starvation and the new diseases that will result, as if AIDS wasn't enough. But there has to be some kind of an answer, even if it's only a partial one. If only people were smaller, then they wouldn't consume so much."

"Hold on a minute Steve. You just said something that really grabbed me - that remark about people being smaller. There may be a way," Alan mumbled, "We've learned a lot about DNA in the last few decades. That old double helix that has governed our development might be usable to make some changes that could prove beneficial. I've been working in genetics now for more than 15 years and it seems that there are some possibilities that have been overlooked todate."

"Just what are you driving at? Surely you aren't aiming to change people. And even if you were, there is no way you can get them to come to some clinic and get shots or whatever that might change them or make their offspring smaller."

"That's for sure, and besides, even if people would take shots that would alter their DNA, there just isn't the time or the facilities throughout the world to make an impact. And what is more, it would take too long, if it didn't prove impossible to educate people to the necessity of change and get them to accept it."

"Some years ago, about 1994, I read a book *The Truth About Your Height* by some guy named Samaras. He thought that people were getting too tall for their own good. Further, Samaras predicted that there would be a devastating environmental effect if Americans kept growing at the same rate as they had for the past 75 years. He claimed that a 20% increase in height would increase energy needs by 50%, require an additional 180 million acres for food production and pump 3 billion extra tons of carbon dioxide into the atmosphere every year. But he did offer a plan. He had no idea of starving kids, but stated that careful monitoring of children's food intake could restrict height by as much as 8 inches. He stated an average height of 5 feet and 110 pounds weight would be about right."

"It sounds like a great idea but it's just too impractical to make it work. Still, I believe that there has to be a way. I just can't accept the concept that God wants to see the world destroyed by the direction it's presently headed." From time to time Steve recalled that conversation, but always shelved it in his mind as the obstacles seemed overwhelming.

When he could get away, Steve visited the old mill site of Minnesota Mines. He arranged with a contractor from Idaho Springs to clear off the debris from the former mining and milling operation. Most of the old structures were falling down after being buried time and again by the heavy winter snows. But the old Gilpin County sorting bin stood like a rock, as good as the day it had been completed. It was located on a side hill close to the portal of the old mine. It was designed so that the mule-trammed one-ton mine cars could be dumped on a grizzly made up of twelve 120# rails spaced eight inches apart. These rails installed with the ball down were about twelve feet long with each end fitted into huge 16 inch by 16 inch timber.

The rails sloped downward at an angle of 37 degrees below the horizontal. At the lower end of the grizzly was a workspace 6 feet wide where men armed with sledge hammers could break up any ore boulders that didn't go through the grizzly. A bin under the grizzly collected all the minus eight inch material. Waste boulders on the grizzly were pulled to one side and dropped into a chute leading to mine cars that could be trammed to a waste dump.

The bottom of the bin sloped at 50 degrees and was fitted with two chutes from which mine cars of minus eight inch ore were loaded and trammed to the nearby mill.

Steve decided to let it stand as a monument to the active mine that once occupied the site and in honor of his remembered grandpa.

When the job of clearing the mill site was done, Steve found he had a level two-acre cabin site that nestled on the east side of a wooded draw. Looking to the north, he could see the ridge of the continental divide. He could spot the location of Berthoud Pass. South he looked over Empire towards Georgetown and the peaks that loomed over the Argentine valley. To the west was a near vertical rock face some 300 ft. wide that rose over 200 ft. to a timbered ridge.

Using the sketches that he and Susan had made so long ago, Steve began and finally finished a small cabin built of logs hauled in from a mill in Idaho Springs. They were flattened on two sides and grooved for a spline to go between each log.

"Alan, I think I can build this cabin all alone. The pioneers often built log cabins by themselves and I think I should be able to so as well."

Steve started the cabin alone, but when he saw how slow the job was going, he employed two men from Empire to help with the job.

Laboriously and using all sorts of jack-leg arrangements, they finally got the walls up for a cabin 24 ft. wide and 32 ft. long. It had no windows nor doors. These were cut in later with a chain saw.

The long ridge pole was put in place using a helicopter. The roof rafters were placed. Treated half-inch plywood made up the base of the split shake roof that topped the one story cabin.

Spring was in the air. With the melting of the winter snows, both Steve and Alan had the yen to get out, to hike and enjoy the awakening of the land and to fish for trout that had a hunger built up in the months of hibernation. Ice still blanketed many lakes but the streams were becoming ice free sooner. It didn't take Steve and Alan very long to decide where they were going and to gather up their gear.

Once the Jeep was ready, they took off for Empire and fished Clear Creek below the Henderson Mine.The trout were ready. They gobbled May flies But there were other hungry bugs that had wintered in hidden places while awaiting Spring. Biting mosquitoes and flies were even more abundant than the hungry trout. When the two made camp that evening, the first action was to get a smoky fire going to fend off the annoying bugs. The fire helped some but the hungry mosquitoes persisted in their efforts to break their long winter fast. Deet, generously applied, helped to deter their buzzing assaults as the insects searched for fresh blood.

Broiled trout, pork and beans and Cole slaw made a meal for the hungry fishermen. After a sour mash nightcap, they settled down for the night and a long sleep that would be interrupted frequently by the biting insects. As Steve lay awake several times during the night, the germ of an idea began to form.

They were wakened during the night by a sudden unpredicted mountain storm. Its violence forced them to the decision to break camp and drive about ten miles to Steve's cabin above Empire. Hail and rain beat down. What a roaring storm! I'm sure glad that you had the foresight to build this place. We're lucky that you cut out the door and a few of the windows so we could get in. I wouldn't want to be stuck out there on a wild night like this. I'll bet that campsite will be under water before morning."

It grew cooler. Sleep was impossible as the lightning flashes and resounding thunder seemed to shake the cabin. The rain came in torrents. "Let's build a fire before we freeze." said Steve. He groped around and came up with a few logs, actually the pieces cut out by making the cabins' door and windows. Soon the crackling flames in the rough stone fireplace began to dispel the damp chill of the cabin. They chatted as the ominous storm seemed to increase in intensity. Finally they collapsed on their sleeping bags and dozed off.

They awoke abruptly to a different sound. The cabin shook as they heard the crash of falling rock. Steve exclaimed, "Boy, am I glad that I built on this side of the valley. With all that rock tumbling off the cliff face, we would have been wiped out if the cabin was too close."

Finally the roar of the storm subsided but the quiet was punctuated by rock that continued to fall from the nearby cliff face. An uneasy sleep overcame the fisherman and they awakened late to a bright shining day.

As he lay there waking, and scratching his insect bites, Steve thought of his ideas of the night before. Even if you could modify chromosomes and DNA, you would never be able to get people to come into a clinic and voluntarily get an injection that might impact on any future offspring. And even if their were hordes of willing people ready to accept the injection that might result in small children there were far more people that could never be reached. It was almost certain that those who were more difficult to reach and who would be most likely to object to the injection would be the people that needed it most.

He dressed, restarted the fire,and went out on the porch to view the beauty of the silent day. To his surprise, the cliff presented a different appearance. The massive rock fall exposed a new cliff face. High up on the fresh surface, Steve saw the dark opening of an old mine drift that had been exposed by the rock fall. Steve woke Alan.

"Hey, old man, time's a'wasting. Get up and see what happened during the night."

Sleepily Alan awoke and dressed and they went out with field glasses to take a closer look at the opening in the new cliff face. There wasn't much to see, just the shadowed cave-like five by seven foot opening that offered no more clues as to its existence.

"That's strange. All the working of Minnesota Mines were on the opposite side of the valley. Someday, I'm gonna' get up there and maybe I can see what they were looking for. I'll need help and more equipment than we have here now. With a long rope, I could climb down that cliff and get in. Actually, two ropes will be needed or one long one that will go from the cliff top to the bottom. I don't want to try to climb back up once I've gotten down to that drift." mused Steve.

Over a breakfast of left-over trout and cold beans, Steve and Alan pursued their discussion of population, genes and intelligence. Steve pointed out,"Those nations that have achieved a reduction in the rate of population growth are those in which the people have higher incomes and a higher social status. They also have a higher IQ than the people of less favored nations. Together with the lower IQ go such social ills as crime, illegitimacy and welfare dependence."

"What is most significant about this," said Alan, "is that IQ is shaped more by genes than by environment and no means have been discovered whereby IQ can be raised significantly."

"You're sure right about that! The situation is getting worse as our misguided welfare policies foster the higher-than-average propagation rate of low IQ people pushing down the nation's average intelligence level at the same time that lower-level jobs are disappearing and social ills are becoming more aggravated."

"What your saying, Al, is that there are getting to be more and more of us and we are getting dumber and dumber. That doesn't bode too well for the human race! It seems clear that there has to be some sort of action taken that would reverse that trend. Something that would reduce the population growth rate particularly among those with the lower IQs and, at the same time, foster the limited growth of the people that have higher IQs."

"That's about it, Steve, but I can't see how in the hell man could ever impose such control. Certainly it gets down to basics that affect the life cycle involving not only sperm count, but altering chromosomes, DNA and genes."

"Oh boy! You left me behind when you brought those things into this discussion. I know about the elements and how they combine to form minerals and how the minerals form rocks,but when you get off into the field of biochemistry and biology, I just don't get it. Isn't there some way you could simplify those terms so that I could grasp them.?"

"Could be, but for the life of me I can't see why I should try to tell you in five minutes what I've spent a lifetime learning. But maybe I'll give it a try. You sure have to understand something about those topics if we are going to look further into this population problem that will, in the end, destroy us! I've got all kinds of books that should be of some help in giving you an understanding of genetics. Wait, I've got a better idea. I have a research associate that might be willing to give you some help."

CHAPTER 2.
A GENETIC SOLUTION ?

"That would be great! I could spend some time with him and maybe get to understand some of these things that have such a powerful impact on who and what we are. It's going to take many hours for me to even begin to grasp that biological stuff that I don't know the first thing about. If I could spend several hours each day with this fellow, perhaps over a beer or so, hopefully I could get an understanding of what make us tick."

"Not so, Chum. In the first place it is not a he but a she. Nina Adams is her name. In the second place we've got to find out if she is willing to put up with a hard-nosed engineer and try to implant some medical knowledge. If Nina is willing maybe it would be best to make a trial run to see if you two are compatible. It sure as hell isn't going to work if you and Nina don't get along."

It would seem, thought Alan, that it was quite important to get the teacher-student relationship between Nina and Steve off on the right foot. Nina was a young researcher on Alan's team, the youngest of the group. A recent graduate with a Ph.D. in microbiology, she was enthusiastic about her work on DNA and put in long hours on her research. Would she be willing to work with a complete neophyte and try to educate him in a field completely foreign to his training? It would be an experiment at best and could come a cropper.

Even the first step posed problems. Alan sensed that a neutral meeting place would have to be picked. It was vital that the first meeting of a mining engineer and a microbiologist take place under the very best of circumstances. One of the many down-town bars or restaurants just didn't seem quite right. Perhaps he could enlist Mary's help to arrange for Steve and Nina to meet under auspicious circumstances. Alan approached Mary with the problem.

Mary said, "Why that's easy. We'll just invite both of them over to dinner. It'll be just as casual as possible. Cocktails before dinner should provide lubrication and then we'll let the rest of the evening take care of itself. Nina and Steve will either hit it off or they won't and in either case, we'll know where the matter stands."

Alan agreed with this approach and Mary proceeded to lay plans for a dinner meeting. "Coming up with a menu isn't going to be easy. I know what Steve likes, but I haven't got a clue what would appeal to Nina. I've met her several times but never for a meal or even a snack. I'll just have to give it a whirl and hope that Nina likes it."

"Maybe it would be better, Mary, to keep the menu on an informal basis. Everybody likes hamburgers and I could broil up a bunch of them out on the patio while everyone is having a drink."

Reluctantly, Mary conceded that he was probably right. Informality could be the clue to Nina and Steve getting to know each other.

Finally the invitations were made and the day came along. Steve arrived at the Muster's a bit early. It seemed as if he were early for almost every commitment. Then there was a knock on the door and Nina Adams was ushered in by Alan and introduced. Nina was a 5 foot 7 inch brunette with deep blue eyes. Her shoulder-length hair framed a face with a broad forehead, high cheekbones, a firm chin and lips that seemed ever ready to smile. She was a beautiful girl with figure and features that would have made her a strong competitor in any beauty contest. Her wavy light-brown hair hung free and bounced off her shoulders as she moved to accept Steve's outstretched hand.

Nina was as graceful as a doe in a wheatfield. If she hadn't picked biology as her field of endeavor, Nina would have made out well in modeling or in the movies. Her slightly uptilted nose and her full lips were both appealing and provocative. The girl would have been a stand-out as a Playboy centerfold!

Steve was pleasantly surprised as he had expected to see a bespectacled drab with a pronounced slouch from bending over and peering into a microscope.

After her long hours in the lab each day wearing a smock with pockets loaded with slides and other stuff, Nina liked to dress up. That evening she wore a creamy silk blouse that revealed more than it concealed. Her Navajo earrings and turquoise naja necklace accented the short dark blue skirt cut just above her knees.

When his initial shock was overcome, Steve greeted the well-endowed researcher with a warm handclasp. He began to look forward to what might be too brief an association with this charming scientist. He hoped that she would not turn him down. It would be a pleasure to work with such a lovely person whether or not she agreed to indoctrinate him into the field of genetics.

The four moved to the Muster's family room and relaxed comfortably to enjoy Mary's canapés and Alan's industrial-strength drinks. Mary believed in healthy snacking and served vegetable strips and a dip while Alan mixed drinks. It turned out that Nina and Steve were both partial to bourbon. After a drink or so they moved out to the patio. The smell of the evergreens scented the early evening air.

Alan had not given Nina a hint about any ulterior motive for their social gathering. He was fearful that Nina would have flatly turned down the idea of her serving as an instructor for some engineer. Now it was entirely up to Steve to sell himself and his ideas to Nina.

Steve knew that Nina had not been forewarned about their meeting having an ulterior purpose. Then, too, he was somewhat overwhelmed by the beauty and charm of this lovely scientist. He yearned to have her concur and to educate him. But how to proceed was both a challenge and a problem. Alan helped by directing their casual small talk in several channels and finally to the over population problem.

This was what Steve was waiting for. "Isn't your particular field of interest concerned with DNA?"

"Yes it is," Nina said, "and I'm so happy that Alan led me into it. It is a wide open field that offers the opportunity to make some beneficial changes for mankind's future well-being."

"Sure wish that I knew more about DNA. It could, possibly, be the answer to the critical problem of over population

"How's that? What are you thinking about?"

This was the opening Steve needed. "Well, when you look at the explosive rate of population growth, especially in the less developed nations, it gets kind of scary."

"I don't understand. Why is it scary?" challenged Nina.

"Every day, in the news, there are items about food shortages, famines and the like. This information, linked to the doubling rate of populations shows that these crises occur mainly in countries where populations are rapidly expanding. Although the world's inhabitants are doubling in 42 years, many countries have doubling rates of half that."

"I never realized that! Why there isn't enough arable land to sustain such growth. What a mess! Is the world doomed to create its own background for a mass extinction?"

"Possibly, but I am hoping that there may be a way to avoid that finale. Perhaps some way can be found to reduce the adverse impact of too many people on too small a planet. The solution may rest with scientists like yourself that have the highly specialized knowledge to genetically alter people."

After that he wasted no time in explaining how their meeting was a prelude to what he hoped would be a series of sessions where she could indoctrinate him into some of the principles of genetics.

Alan interjected, "I hope you look favorably on this idea, Nina, as Steve has a few ideas that might be furthered if he had a basic understanding of genetics."

"Why do you want to get into a subject that is so very different than engineering?" asked Nina.

"It just isn't the easiest thing to explain. I've been doing a lot of reading, some of it the charts and papers published by the Population Reference Bureau and from many other sources. When I see population doubling rates of twenty-five years and less, well, frankly I'm scared. Many parts of the world are short of food now and to think that the world will have twice as many people in just forty more years scares the hell out of me. It just seems that something has to be done and soon!"

"You know, Steve, I've been so busy in my own little world of research that I just never have thought about the problem you've outlined. The way you put it, it sort of frightens me too."

"I can understand how over population hasn't been on your mind. This situation reminds me of the story about the difference between an engineer and a scientist. It goes something like this 'An engineer is someone who knows less and less about more and more until he finally knows nothing about everything, but a scientist knows more and more about less and less until he finally knows everything about nothing.' That's probably an exaggeration but it illustrates the different viewpoints of the two fields."

"OK, Steve. I'm not sure that I can give you what you want to know in a reasonable amount of time, but I'm willing to give it a try for a few weeks. Then let's look at where we are and see if it's worthwhile continuing." It was agreed that they meet in Denver for dinner. With Nina living in Littleton and Steve in Evergreen, to meet in the city seemed appropriate.

"That's just great! Since I'm gonna' be the prime beneficiary of these meetings, the tab is on me. And I think I should pay you for your time as well."

"OK, I'll be happy for you to grab the dinner tabs. We can talk about my time later."

Further, they decided that the first meeting would be in the dining room of the Brown Palace Hotel rather than in one of the many more intimate sites in the city. At their first mid-week meeting, Nina wasted no time in getting into the subject as they sipped their cocktails.

"Genetics is the science concerned with the study of biological inheritance with the gene being the basic unit of inheritance. From here on, the subject gets complex. By the way, Steve, when you were in college, did you have a course in organic chemistry?"

"No, I didn't. All the things I have had to deal with, minerals, rocks how to mine them and how to recover specific minerals from an ore are concerned with inorganic chemistry. So my education lacked any training in the field of organic chemistry."

"That's too bad, as having organic chemistry in your background would make it easier for you to understand the complexities of biochemistry. What we need to discuss in genetics is almost entirely based on biochemistry.

"If we are to understand living organisms, especially man, biochemistry is the essential background for grasping the massive body of existing knowledge that is constantly being augmented by a torrent of brilliant discoveries. Biochemistry describes the origin of form. The chemical constituents and their interrelationships establish the microscopic anatomy - the nature of cells and the forces involved in their association with other cells. Biochemistry describes heredity including information on the nature and behavior of an organism that is passed on from generation to generation. Further,biochemistry is involved with the inevitable aging process."

Steve wasn't overwhelmed, but sagely commented, "I can see that this isn't going to be easy. If I'm going to get to the meat of this business, I can see that I'll have to hit the books and do some homework!"

"That's true! I have some college course books that could be helpful. I'll bring them along when we meet again." Steve took this offer promptly and was inwardly delighted that it seemed to indicate that Nina had embraced the idea of instructing him. He would have liked to embrace her.

Each week hours passed as Nina explored DNA, chromosomes and the structural and metabolic disorders that are passed on to children through their parent's chromosomes and the hundreds of genes each chromosome carries. She explained in detail the efforts of Gregor Mendel whose work in breeding garden peas led him to formulate three laws: the principle of segregation, the purity of gametes, and the mathematical ratio of possible combinations. Nina stated how Mendel's work done in the garden of a monastery was ignored until about 1900.

"DNA," explained Nina, "is much more than it appears. It is made up of four basic kinds of particles: guanine, adenosine, thymine and cytosine. With a single gene made up of some 250,000 of such particles, it takes a lot of hunting to find a specific particle that may be the reason for a person's height, color or other characteristic."

Steve was appalled. "How can you ever get down to things so small?"

"It isn't easy! There is lots to do just to get to the DNA. A blood sample is diluted with sugar water and spun in a high speed centrifuge to separate the red cells from the white cells. The part of the sample containing the red cells is drained off and buffers added. More centrifuging and the addition of other specifics. Then you can eventually see the tangled fine white threads of DNA suspended in a clear liquid.

"You know something about heredity. Some of your features were inherited from your dad and others came from your mom. Those characteristics were established when the mobile male gamete, the sperm, joined with the immobile female gamete, the ovum. The genes in the chromosomes established your physical traits, but some complex traits such as intelligence were modified, in part, by the environment in which you were raised."

"Hold on for just a cotton pickin' minute. You've already left me behind. Tell me more about those chromosomes."

Nina smiled . "Stop me anytime I'm going too fast. This topic isn't the easiest one in the world, but it is one that you have to have a good grasp of if you're ever going to get anywhere with your grand plan. Now let's get back to those chromosomes. Actually they are thread-like bundles in the nuclei of the cells of bodies of organisms. They carry the genes that determine heredity. Chromosomes are arranged in pairs, and the number of pairs is constant within a given species.We humans normally have 46 chromosomes arranged in 23 pairs. One of each pair is passed on to offspring during reproduction. They look like an elongated X with a narrow angle between the limbs."

"OK, I think I can grasp that. But it comes as a shock to learn that what I thought was a biologic act instigated by emotion , turns out to be a biochemical process."

Nina smiled and went on to explain how genes, biochemical substances in the chromosomes, encoded the hereditary information that determines individual char-acteristics.

"Genes are made up from building blocks called DNA, a chemically complex double-helix shaped substance that is the basis for genetic organization in both plants and animals. And here is the clue to your goals. DNA is the basis of genetic organization in both plants and animals. Using recombinant DNA techniques, one or more genes from one species can be inserted into the DNA of another species enabling it to produce the protein encoded by that gene."

But all their hours together were not spent in deliberate instruction. Steve was enchanted with his lovely teacher and listened eagerly to her dissertations while he admired her pert nose, mobile lips and well-groomed hair. Her well-formed figure drew his attention at every opportunity,

On inquiry, Nina told a bit about herself. "I was born and raised in Las Cruces, New Mexico, where I had many opportunities with my folks to hike and camp in the Organ Mountains and the Mogollons. With two older brothers to watch over me I led a rather sheltered life. But all the times were good times! After I got my degree from New Mexico A & M in Cruces. I knew that I wanted to go on. So I came north and earned my Ph.D. at Boulder."

Some weeks later, Steve allowed, "What you've been telling me is exactly what I need to know to further explore the theory I've come up with. If only people were smaller, then the world's resources would go much further. Hence I needed some understanding as to why the Bushmen of the Kalahari desert in Botswana and the Pygmies on Luzon and in the African rain forest are the way they are. But I can see that environment is also a potent factor. For example the changes in the diet of the Japanese is fostering a trend to increased height in the younger generations."

"Not only the environment but many ingested substances can modify an otherwise normal fetus. In addition to unwanted viral or bacterial infections, voluntarily ingested substances such as tobacco, alcohol and possibly even caffeine are potentially harmful. Drugs,legal,illegal,precription and over-the counter can also cause birth defects. By the same token genetic engineering could be utilized to effect changes in a fetus ."

"I recently saw something about genetic engineering," commented Steve, "about how genes were pinpointed that were linked to a number of human ailments such as Lou Gehrig's disease, colon cancer, hyperactivity and to enable sketching the first rough map of all human chromosomes. Is research going on to explore ways to replace damaged genes?"

"That's right and the research in genetics is expanding it's horizons continuously. As early as 1993, bits of DNA were extracted from the bone marrow of a 65 million year old *Tyrannosaurus Rex* and intact DNA was recovered from an insect trapped in amber back in the Mesozoic era, 130 million years ago."

"In this field of genetic engineering, where progress has already been made in the modification and improvement of some farm animals, would it be possible to genetically engineer smaller people?"

"I think so, but little has been done so far towards changing people. Most of the effort has gone into pinpointing genes that are linked to major ailments. But it's only a short step to arrive at the engineering of genes that would alter people's physical characteristics."

"Suppose one wanted to shoot at the target of modifying human characteristics, just how would you go about it?".

"I'm not sure, but I suppose the first thing to do might be the study of the DNA and genes of people that have been historically small for many generations. That means studying blood samples from those Kalahari Bushmen and the Pygmies of Luzon and the Ituri rain forest. Getting such samples wouldn't be easy!"

Steve and Nina continued their sessions for several months as they dined in many of Denver's fine restaurants.

They became more comfortable with one another as they delved into the mysteries of genetics. "Let's go back to those chromosomes for a bit. As I told you, they vary in size and shape and usually come in pairs. Most cells in the human body contains 23 pairs of chromosomes. Each cell contains many genes with each gene located at a particular site on the chromosome.

"The process of cell division results in most of the cells having identical sets of genes. This is called mitosis and every time a chromosome divides into two equal parts, the two parts travel to opposite ends of the cell. Each cell thus formed has the same array of chromosomes and genes as the original."

"When humans and other higher organisms reproduce sexually, special sex cells called gametes are produced by a unique kind of cell division called meiosis.

"Do you know what a zygote is, Steve?"

" Hmmm, I'm not sure. Is it a Hungarian dance?"

"Now you are trying to be funny. No it's not a dance of any kind. It is what is formed when two gametes unite in fertilization. The zygote contains the full, double set of chromosomes. Normally half of these chromosomes will come from one parent and half from the other."

"Do you really think I need to know all this? It seems like we may be going to a depth that may not be germane to the main concept."

"Not at all, Steve.The things we are getting into are absolutely vital to any understanding of evolution and why people are the way they are. If we are going to find out why short people are short, it will be through an appraisal of their heredity and their genetic makeup.

"When gametes unite, two sets of genes are brought together, one set from each parent. Each gene in a specific site on a chromosome affects a particular trait and is represented by two copies, one from each parent. When these copies are identical the individual is homozygous for that particular gene. But when they're different because each parent has contributed a different form, or allele, of the same gene, the individual is said to be heterozygous for that particular gene."

"Now you can understand, Steve, why all this information is vital to determining why small people are small. Further it means that a blood sample from 'small' people must be subjected to a tremendous amount of analysis to identify the the precise genes and alleles that accomplish certain effects on individuals. But it can be done."

"Now you have brought up something new. What is an allele?"

"Oh my! It seems like we'll have to go over this again and again in order to grasp it. But here it is. Every gene carries alleles in its genetic material. There may be many of these alleles. They detarmine the ability of a person to form pigment in the skin, the hair, and the eyes for example. Some alleles are dominant and are designated with a capital letter such as A. A recessive gene would be designated with a small a. Each parent contrubutes alleles to their offspring.

Heterozygous persons (Aa) as well as persons homozygous (AA) for the pigment producing allele have normal pigmentation. Persons homozygous for the allele that results in a lack of pigment (aa) are albinos. The action of genes is seldom a simple matter of a single gene controlling a single trait."

All of their conversations did not dwell solely on their prime target. Now and then they would dine at a place where slow dance music added to the atmosphere.

"That was a fine dinner and I'm full." murmured Nina as they relaxed with an after-dinner drink. "Let's dance?" Nina rose and Steve was delighted to hold her warm and shapely figure in his arms as they stepped and swayed to the seductive music. It must have been enjoyable to Nina too as she urged further dances.

As her curves pressed against him, Steve drank in the fragrance of her hair and body. Neither was Nina immune to the strong male presence of Steve. As they held one another in a warm and tight embrace, they moved to the slow cadence of the waltz and both wanted the moments to linger. But the song ended and they returned to their table.

"As much as I am enjoying our evenings of instruction and your company," Steve allowed, "it seems that we have reached the point where we should be getting some samples of blood in order to proceed."

"No it isn't Steve. There is much more that you need to know before we are ready for samples."

"Such as?"

"We've only touched the surface of the field of genetics. We need to get into how genes affect traits such as weight, height and degree of pigmentation.These factors usually depend on many genes in addition to the influemce of the environment. Frequently the effect of certain genes appears to be additive whereby each gene seems to produce a small increment or decrement independent of other genes.

"We must spend some time on the complex processes by which organisms are diversified and modified through sustained changes in form and function. You remember reading Darwin's famous book *On the Origin of Species by Means of Natural Selection* don't you?"

"No. I never did read his book although I've heard a lot about it. I was too busy studying mineralogy and geological texts."

"Well, Steve, you have to read it now for it is the landmark, the pillar of wisdom, in our understanding of nature. Darwin observed that although offspring inherit a resemblance to their parents, they are not identical to them.

Darwin noted that some of the differences between parents and their offspring were not due solely to the environment but were often inheritable.

"You know how animal breeders are able to change the characteristics of domestic animals by selecting for breeding those individuals with the most desireable qualities such as speed in racehorses or trail scenting in dogs. Artificial selection creates these changes while natural selection promotes the survival of those most fit to tolerate environmental changes. Such changes take place over many generations and explains why the 'small' people of the earth are that way.

"This concept of natural selection has been challenged by those who felt that mutationism was a more realistic theory. The supporters of this concept had discovered that inheritable changes in genes or mutations could occur spontaneously and randomly without regard to the environment. In developing this science of population genetics, several geneticists working independently showed that, even when a mutation that is immediately favored appears, its subsequent spread within a population depends on a number of variables such as the size of the populations, the length of generations, the degree to which the mutation is favorable and the rate at which the same mutation reappears in descendants.

"I do hope you can understand all of this as these things are essential to what we'll be getting into as we process those blood samples that we plan to get."

"I think I'm getting a bit of a glimmer of light on the subject. Nina, I can see that your mind is full of much more than you have spoken about. In time I would hope that my understanding might increase. The world needs the smaller people that we'll be striving for. But even beyond that goal, there is a need to reduce the proliferation of the 'smaller' folk as well. Families must shrink in size if we are to avoid a world that, in time, could become overpopulated with small people But at this point in time, getting a grasp of why the small people are that way is our first objective and that means we must get the blood samples that we need to examine."

CHAPTER 3
THE KALAHARI

Going abroad to seek a sample of blood from little people was a major forward step and one that would require considerable coordination and funding. Steve and Nina met with Alan to review the matter.

"For several months now, Nina has been my teacher and I feel that I've made real progress in learning about how people are different and the related why. I think we're ready to go on to the next step and obtain blood samples of little people and go onto the analytical phase. This ain't gonna' happen unless you can finance the effort! How about it Alan?"

"That's just great! I'm glad you've made such progress. I kind of thought that you would be wanting to get some blood samples. But what are we talking about in terms of time and money? My budget is limited and I don't want to get into something that could be open ended and then find that it had to be cut off too soon."

"We have been discussing the time and dollars part of the problem and feel that $50,000 should be sufficient to get started and to carry the program far enough along to be able to attract such additional financing as might be needed. That initial sum should be enough for us to get the samples we need and do enough work to develop a recombinant DNA that could be proven with mice as a means of size reduction."

"I think you may have underestimated your requirements. Neither you nor Nina have been involved in financing a research program. There are always unexpected things that come up and they always require money. But I can go along with you and will go as far as $75,000 over the next twelve months."

It didn't take long for Steve and Nina to arrange their schedules. "We need enough time to get to Botswana and get into the Kalahari desert."

"Doesn't that mean we go first to Capetown and then kind of backtrack north?"

"Not quite, Nina. I've been looking at schedules a bit and if we time our travel right, we can fly to Johannesburg and then go overland to Botswana."

They agreed that three weeks should be enough time to travel to Botswana, trek the Kalahari, contact a tribe of Bushmen, get the samples and return to Denver. Provision had to be made to keep blood samples refrigerated from the time of taking to their arrival in the controlled conditions of Alan Muster's laboratory..

Getting ready for the trip was complex. Clothing, food, shelter, sleeping bags, camping gear and sampling equipment had to be obtained. They had to accumulate items that would appeal to the Bushmen and help persuade them to cooperate in allowing their blood samples to be taken.

Steve did some research on the Bushmen and found they had absolutely no use for money. In general, things were just surplus baggage. Their habit was to wander through the Kalahari Desert with the main objective of survival. The tribes were small, usually consisting of three or four families for a population of 20 to 25 persons. The Bushmen's diet was diverse. Small antelope and rodents and even lizards and bugs all contributed to the meager fare of the tribe.The tribe owned no land and had the minimum of encumbrances, usually the clothes on their back, their weapons, a few utensils for cooking and to carry water and animal skins to protect them from the chill of the desert nights.

With no fixed residence, or even an area to call home, the Bushmen wandered at will over the vastness of the Kalahari. The 100,000 square mile area of the Kalahari is close to the area of Virginia, Maryland and Pennsylvania combined. Bushmen contacts with other tribes were few and far from pleasant as the Bushmen were looked down upon as an inferior species by the Namib, Ohekwe, Nusan and several other tribes that populated the borders of the Kalahari desert.

Alan was kept informed on the progress of Steve's indoctrination in the field of genetics as well as the travel plans.

"While you're in that part of the world, I think you should plan on getting blood samples from the Pygmies of the rain forest. That could be harder than the job of work you've got to handle in the Kalahari. There you can at least see for some distance as you seek out Bushmen. But in the Ituri rain forest, or any other rain forest that may be a host for Pygmies, you have to travel on foot and your vision will be limited by the thick tangled jungle. See how your time and money goes and take it from there. But it would be better if you could include some Pygmy blood samples too."

"I know you're right. We do need some Pygmy blood. But with the limited staff and all the work that has to be done on a sample to find out what limits their height, would the Pygmy blood sample still be usable if it has to sit around for a few months?"

"Good question, Steve. But we have means of storage at the right temperatures and all so that a blood sample may be kept indefinitely. But you two are tackling the field work and it will be your judgment that will be the basis for a decision."

It was finally decided to defer approaching the African Pygmies until a later date. At least in the Kalahari Desert, it would be feasible to travel with a Land Rover. Great distances could be covered in acceptable times as the pair searched for an amenable tribe of Bushmen. Several cables and overseas telephone calls served to locate a used Land Rover that appeared to suit their needs.

At a memorable evening at the Muster home in Evergreen, the four laid final plans for the African safari to contact the Bushmen. Departing Denver International airport Nina and Steve would fly to Dulles to change planes for the flight to Casablanca to rest up for a day or two at the El Mansour hotel before flying to Johannesburg. There, again, a few days rest and provisioning for the desert trek would be followed by travel to Gabarone in Botswana, the departure point in the search for a Bushmen tribe.

The problem of taking the sample and preservation of the blood until its arrival in the lab came in for much discussion.

"Have you all got it figured out just how you are going to take a sample and get it into the refrigerated box?" asked Alan.

"Why no we haven't. But it can't be too difficult, can it?" posed Steve.

"I can see we have some work to do! For the next several days you two are going to get indoctrinated in the business of taking blood samples. I'm going to make arrangements for you both to work at Denver General Hospital where your principal occupation will be to take blood samples. You'll train under the direction of an RN who will make sure that you know just how to do the job before she lets you try on your own. Nina knows something about the process already but you'll both be experts within several days."

Sue and Steve learned fast. They learned how to tap veins and arteries and how to select needle sizes according to their victims special requirements. After the first day, they were tired of seeing blood. By the end of the second day, the sample taking and care was second nature to them.

Nina postulated, "This is easy when the patient is willing. But what if we get into a stuation where we have the person we need to sample, but he or she objects? How in the world can we get a sample from an unwilling target?"

"That could sure happen! I have a life-sized picture of you, Nina, chasing a Bushman around with a needle in your hand while the Bushman leads you a merry chase in the desert with his loin-cloth flapping as he runs across the sand."

Over coffee in the nurses lounge, Steve broached this subject to several of the nurses. One jokingly suggested a rubber hammer.

None of the nurses had ever encountered a completely unwilling patient although all had experience with reluctant ones. They finally decided that the two trekkers would need a tranquilizing gun to make sure that a blood sample might be had from an unwilling subject.

As soon as the sample was taken it would be necessary to keep it in a specially insulated container chilled with dry ice to assure its arrival in Denver in an unaltered condition. By radio telephone it was determined that dry ice was obtainable in Johannesburg.

Finally the departure date arrived and both Nina and Steve looked forward to the trip as a great adventure. Neither had been to Africa before. Their flight left Dulles in the evening.

"Which seat do you want?" asked Steve. Let's toss a coin to see who gets to choose." Nina won and slid into the window seat. Nina spent a lot of time looking out leaving Steve free to look at her without her knowing.

He thought, "How did I ever get so lucky to get such a beautiful traveling companion? And smart too. The last few months have been extraordinary. I've learned about things I never dreamed that I'd get into. But will it work? Will our efforts result in smaller people? Will the world be changed for the better as a result?" Only time, hard work, yes, and money too, would ever let them find out.

Sleep finally came to Steve when they were far out over the Atlantic. Their arms touched and he could feel her movements as Nina breathed softly. Moving eastward at 600 mph, the length of darkness was too brief.

Nina was the first to waken. She turned and looked at Steve who was still dozing. Nina thought, "What am I doing going off an a jaunt like this with a man whom I've only known a few months. We'll be going out in the desert miles and miles away from anything. He is handsome, thoughtful and kind. What's more he has a great idea that may, just may, have a chance of becoming reality. But how are we going to get along. But being alone together in complete isolation may not be the thing to enhance a girl's reputation. However, the die is cast and there's no going back!"

After a restless night they could see the low green line of the Moroccan coast in the early dawn. They landed at Nouasseur airport after overflying the white houses of the three million people that lived in what is called Dar al'Beida in Arabic, the second largest city in Africa. A prearranged van awaited them. They cleared customs and immigration and were soon on their way on the 35 km ride north to Casablanca.

Shortly they passed through the outskirts of Casablanca and to the downtown area where they checked into separate rooms at the modern hotel el Mansour. A good sleep restored their energy and had them looking forward to the trip to the other end of Africa. That evening they went to the restaurant La Mer in the El Hank lighthouse area for dinner. Sipping a fine Montrachet that supplemented the meal they watched the south Atlantic waves roll in and discussed plans for their venture into the unknown Kalahari.

"How will we ever communicate with the Bushmen when and if we find them?"

"It's a cinch we're not going to have any words that they'll understand. Sign language will be our only option. That and your winning smiles ought to get the job done. We'll just have to improvise 'till we find something that works."

Nina looked grim as she commented, "We just have to do better then that. Surely there are some people in Botswana that speak English who are capable of talking with the Bushmen. I think we'd better check around Gabarone and find one of those guys!"

"Gosh, I never though of that. It's a good idea but it means we'll have to have more food, water and shelter."

With a few days to spare before their flight to Johannesburg, Steve rented a car and they drove to Marrakech to overnight at the Hotel Mamounia and see the many wonders of this ancient city at the foot of the Atlas mountains. This was a new and strange culture that they found interesting to explore. A visit to the El Kotubia tower failed to reveal the unique properties attributed to this Moroccan shrine.

As they spent more time together, Steve and Nina both found their association a pleasant one that seemed to be ripening quickly into something more than the teacher-student relationship of their initial alliance.

On their return to Casa Blanca and El Mansour, they checked and rechecked their gear. The next day they checked again to make certain that all their baggage was on board the flight south to Johannesburg. It was a tiring non-stop flight almost the length of the continent.

For only minutes after takeoff they were able to see the sparse green fields of Morocco and the bare expanse of the Atlas mountains as the plane climbed to its assigned altitude. Then a panoply of clouds obscured their view of earth. They seemed suspended in unending space.

Steve turned to Nine saying, "For some time I've been wondering about this business of gene identification. When you get into the task of trying to determine the effect of different genes on the host body, just how much do we really know?"

"Actually, we know a great deal. Those genes are located on the chromosomes like beads on a string. Once it was thought that it took mainly clean living including a proper diet, exercise and the like and longevity would be increased. But that isn't the whole story. Years ago studies were made of groups of centenarians to determine the reason for their longevity. It was found that at least a part of the reason was the presence of two genes. One of these was called APOE. However if you had the misfortune to get the wrong version, you could be subject to Alzheimer's and high cholesterol. Further, the century-old types were more likely to have a particular version of the ACE gene that influences blood pressure.

"The Bushmen that we're going to look for must have some special genes that impart their peculiar characteristics. It's gonna' be a totally different ball game to analyze their blood as opposed to the run-of-the-mill samples I've been studying."

"It isn't just the height of the Bushmen that we'll be dealing with." commented Steve, "The tribe is characterized as being an average of 4 to 4 ½ feet tall but also by their leathery yellow skin and their large buttocks. Seems like quite a task to separate out the genes that affect height and not get a carry over of the genes that make for the Bushmen's big butts. We wouldn't want to inflict more than a lower height on future generations. However, it would be nice if we could modify the greed factors in mankind and improve intellect at the same time. One thing that is almost mandatory is to modify the male sperm count of future generations so that the over- population crisis would be history."

A prearranged Land Rover was waiting for them at the airport in Johannesburg. Once loaded with all the gear, Steve and Nina took off immediately for the 165 mile trip to Gabarone in Botswana. The Land Rover was specially equipped for desert travel. It had oversize tires to enable travel on sand. Water tanks assured an adequate supply for several weeks. Food lockers were built in with gasket seals to exclude bugs.

Steve and Nina were entranced by the scenery as they drove north from Johannesburg. Ever the mining engineer, Steve commented, "Look at the size of those tailings piles! Those huge mounds of white sands are the residue of millions of tons of ore that have been mined and processed for the recovery of the contained gold. Then, beginning in the early 1950's they were reproccessed to recover the pyrite. The pyrite was burned to make sulphur dioxide which was converted into sulphuric acid that was used to leach the tailings to extract the uranium. It was a complex operation but generated a lot of uranium for power production and weapons."

Both had read about the Boers and the battles for their home land and the struggles they had to survive in this vast and arid landscape punctuated by kopjes and mesas. The narrow track of unpaved road through the bushveld wasn't conducive to speed and gave the pair more time to drink in the landscape so foreign to their experience. Clumps of Acacia and Zizyphus trees seemed like islands in the vast expanse. The sun bore down ceaselessly. A few clouds of fleecy white floated slowly across the deep blue South African sky. The horizon was far away with near unending space stretched before the travelers.

Now and then they passed lone travelers and groups of natives walking alongside the road. Either Nina or Steve would wave at the weary people. Their waves were returned but none of the many footsore travelers either asked for or expected a lift. It took four hours for the trip to Gabarone. Tired and covered with dust, the pair sought a place where they could clean up and get some rest.

After some searching on the unpaved streets of the town, they finally came across the Gabarone Hotel a crumbling wood structure across the dirt road from the train station At $12 per night they didn't expect much and were not disappointed. After bucket baths, they closed the unlockable doors of their tiny rooms and collapsed on rusty cots.

Morning came too soon as they woke to the chatter of native Botswanans moving like columns of army ants through the tall grass and thornbrush that surrounded the town. Most of the men were dressed in garish shirts and non-descript pants if they wore pants at all. The women were clothed, at least partially, in bright colored clothes.

All seemed to carry some kind of a burden on their heads-anything from a bundle of firewood to a fruit basket that might be peddled to the coach travelers on the train north to Francistown.

Wood smoke from hundreds of cooking fires laid a haze over the town that sprawled near the foot of some rocky hills. The smoke curled up from the many shanties built of misshapen mud brick, old planks, corrugated tin and even card board. Beer can patches covered some of the dwellings.

A short distance away a few three and four story structures rose above a street of small shops and the mud and thatch daub and wattle huts called rondavels. The awestruck strangers gravitated towards the high buildings a few blocks away in their search for the US Consul. There they met a young man from Oklahoma. This Mr. Owens greeted them with a southwestern drawl that was music to their ears after their few days of only the chatter-like language of the Africans.

One of their first orders of business was to find an interpreter who could converse with the Bushmen in their Khoisan dialect and who was capable of speaking enough English for Steve and Nina to understand.

"We expect to be out in the Kalahari for a week or two searching for some Bushmen whom we can persuade to part with some blood. The job could be a heck of a lot easier if there was a way we could talk to the Bushmen and we hoped you might put us in touch with someone who spoke English as well as Khoisan."

"We don't get many requests like that. Few people even want to go into the Kalahari and those that do don't want to have anything to do with Bushmen. There have been a few photographers that tried to get pictures. More often than not the Bushmen took off. They didn't want their pictures taken. But I may be able to help you. There is a character called Po who might be willing to go, if the price is right. I'll get hold of him and we can find out. How can I get in touch with you so we can arrange a meeting?'

"We are staying at the Gabarone Hotel. It has a few amenities, and a telephone at the desk is one. Just give us a call and leave a message. I'll check often and get back to you."

A few hours later they got the message that Po had been located and that they should meet at the Consulate at three that afternoon.

Po turned out to be a scrawny individual wearing a smelly bright-colored shirt, dirty britches and a patch covering one eye. The visible orb looked sort of sneaky but the Consul assured them that their choice was limited to this single unsavory interpreter. Few had contact with the Bushmen and they should consider themselves lucky in having Po.

Po promised faithfully to be on hand bright and early for the trek into the Kalahari. Steve gave him ten US dollars to bind the deal, probably a big mistake as that sum represented several months of average earnings.

It had been hot that day with the temperature rising to 90° F. To their pleasant surprise the nighttime temperature dropped to 62° F typical of the daytime-nighttime differences in desert climes. It was mid August, close to the end of the brief winter with accompanying showers.

It was about 250 miles to the western edge of the Kalahari where the desert occupied parts of eastern Namibia. Tentatively, Steve and Nina planned to head west for several hundred miles, then make a 50 mile dogleg to the north and then back to Gabarone. Despite the sparse population, they hoped to intercept some of the few thousand Bushmen that clung to the desert. Just in case they needed to make local purchases or pay for anything in local currency they went to one of the banks in Gabarone, capital city of Botswana, and exchanged some dollars for pula at the rate of 2.15 pula per dollar. The colorful pula bills were attractive as were the several denominations of coins. Both bills and coins featured the varied wildlife of the region.

All was ready as they awaited their trusty interpreter. But he never appeared and the two trekkers decided to move out regardless. They were loaded up with everything they could think of including food, extra gas, a .38 revolver for each and both a .22 rifle and a .308 equipped with four-power telescopes. They had plenty of dry ice in well-insulated containers for the Bushmen blood samples they sought. They made a last call on Mr. Owens

"Po never showed up, so we're headed out anyhow." Steve exclaimed.

"I kinda' thought that might happen. He's probably sleeping off a fine six-pack headache. These folk just can't handle having so much money at one time." confided Mr. Owens.

"Tell us how to get started into the Kalahari."

"Head southwest on the road to Kanye which is about 50 miles out. There the road ends but there are ways out to the Kalahari if you can follow the tracks or spoors. When you get to Kanye look up a character named Phil Emerson. He's lived there for years. How he has survived is beyond me but he always has enough money for tobacco and booze. He knows the country and can put you on the right track for the Kalahari."

It was ten in the morning when they finally got underway and headed southwest to Kanye. The dirt road wasn't much and they bogged down a few times in the mud left by the recent winter rains. Stuffing lots of thornbrush under the wheels. got them out of several mirings and by early afternoon they were in Kanye. Kanye was an accumulation of rondavels, the near-round mud and wattle single-room dwellings so common in all of southern Africa.

They found Phil Emerson seated on a bench outside his rondavel. His tattered straw hat offered little protection for his bulbous red nose. A spattered mud colored open shirt and equally non-descript frayed pants completed his attire. A big Rhodesian Ridgeback sat at his side and growled ominously at the strangers A half-dozen kids of assorted hues and sizes played in the dust.

Two native women attended him as Emerson rose to greet Steve and Nina.

"Howdy and welcome. We don't get to see strangers very often. You're the first in over a year. Stay and set a spell." They knew they had to indulge Emerson and chatted for a while.

The varicolored children watched Nina with wide-eyed curiosity. Never before had they seen a white woman. One reached out with her forefinger and gently traced it down

The Pringle Progression   57

Nina's arm. To her surprise, the white color didn't rub off. Nina thought to herself, "Could we create a race of blond-headed blue-eyed blacks or whites with kinky black hair?" More importantly. she pondered, "Seals have a bone in their male sex organs and the walrus is blessed with an Oosick. What about altering man to have a bony center in his penis? Then never again would there be an impotence problem?"

"What brings you to Kanye?'

"We really didn't really plan a visit to Kanye as we're headed for the Kalahari."

"I can't see why anyone would want to go out there!" said Emerson as he motioned to one of the colorfully dressed women to fill his pipe. She did so and lit the strong tobacco with a twig from a smoldering fire. She took a few puffs and handed the pipe back to Emerson.

"There's bugger-all out there but miles and miles of bloody Africa."

"We're here to get a few Bushmen blood samples and plan to wander in the Kalahari till we can come across some willing donors."

"That's a rough go! There aren't but a few Bushmen out there and they move around constantly looking for something to eat and drink."

"How do we get started?" asked Steve, anxious to bring the confrontation to a close.

"Out of town down thataway, there's a faint track but you should be able to follow it. When you come to a large acacia broken off about 10 feet up. turn right and follow the spoor. You're in the Kalahari then for sure."

From semi-arid there was a rapid change to arid as the Land Rover moved westward into the sandveld. The sun blazed and everything seemed bathed in a brassy glow. The temperature rose quickly to 95° F as they followed what appeared to be a traveled footpath. But then they came to a six foot drop-off and had to retreat to find a way into what appeared to be a dry wash. Dry it was and no mistake. From the scrub brush that surrounded Kanye, they had passed into a beige-colored rocky area with windblown sands all around.

What did manage to grow in this strange land was thorny. Each variety harbored its own particular brand of nature's hypodermic needle. Some had black shiny quills that penetrated deeply into the flesh before you knew it. This was truly a hostile landscape Even the seed burrs bit!

Topping a rise, they were startled to see a host of some eight or ten Meerkats. They stood on their hind legs forming a two-foot high mass of grayish fur. Steve stopped the Land Rover. The Meerkats peered at the intruders. Their large brown eyes had a disapproving, resentful look. With their forepaws held in front of their stomachs and pointed towards their feet, they were a somber disgruntled group. Soon they dropped to their all fours and scampered swiftly out of sight.

Ten miles into the Kalahari, the trekkers stopped to look around. A cool drink would have been refreshing as the constant dry desert winds seemed to suck the moisture out of their bodies. They settled for the tepid tasteless stuff that passed for water in Botswana.

They walked to a nearby promontory, sat and viewed their surroundings. Low hills, sand dunes and here and there a scruffy bush was all there was. Closer inspection with binoculars revealed no signs of life. They took another path back to the Land Rover. Nina was in the lead when she exclaimed.

"Look at those foot prints! They're big enough to be a lion's."

"Yes, and they probably are. Hand me the camera."

Nina turned and stepped towards Steve with the camera in her extended hand as she walked over both footprints, neatly obliterating them. They both laughed. They moved slowly as their glances took in the surrounding desert searching for any signs of life. They spotted a small antelope that bounded out of sight without a backward glance. A few lizards were observed but did not appear threatening. No snakes were seen as they were most likely coiled in shady crevices out of the heat of the mid-day sun.

About five in the afternoon, they stopped to make camp for the night. Each had a translucent pop-up two-man tent. Steve had a red one and Nina's was blue. They were simple to operate. Only a few empty half-gallon tins filled with sand in lieu of stakes were needed to keep them from blowing away in the near constant winds that swept the barren desert.

Dinner was a simple meal, canned peas and corn plus an antelope steak for each. These had been acquired in Gabarone along with a few other fresh foods that would be used in the first few days of their trek. After that it would be canned goods and biltong. A bottle of wine warmed them both as the chill of the desert night came over the land like a blanket when the sun dropped from view. It was still early when they both retired to their respective tents and sleeping bags .

Morning came too soon, but they finally tumbled out, this time dressed for the part. Both had donned safari suits and desert helmets. Despite the sameness of their dress nothing could conceal the feminine curves that Nina revealed as she bustled about getting their breakfast. Their gear was packed, tents folded and soon they were on the way west guided only by the sun at their back and the compass on the dashboard of the Land Rover.

As they moved slowly west on this second day of their trek they scanned frequently and fruitlessly for signs of Bushmen. They did manage to discover some old Bushmen campsites revealed by the ring of rocks and a few blackened twigs from their campfires. The trekkers knew their task was difficult for there were so few Bushmen remaining in the Kalahari. Many had opted to leave the desert and had been absorbed and interbred with tribes that inhabited the desert's boundary lands. Wherever the solitary Bushmen lived, they left behind skillful drawings on rock walls depicting themselves and the Kalahari animal life.

On this second day of the journey, they traveled a bit later. A rising moon assured them they would have no difficulty in making camp. dinner. For the second time they ate provisions from Gabarone. Then it was bedtime as each retired to their tents for the night.

Steve awoke to a piercing scream as Nina gave vent to her fright. He grabbed a rifle and rushed out. He approached Nina's tent with care and saw a huge mamba waving back and forth close to the tent. A few shots from the .22 rifle finished off the deadly snake. "I thought the mamba was only found in the tropics.".

Nina was shaking from her experience.

"I don't know what woke me, but when I did I saw the moon-cast shadow of the snake waving on the tent wall. I could hardly breath. I needed your help and finally managed to get out that scream. There is no way,"she exclaimed," that I'm going back in that tent.

"They always travel in pairs and I don't want to relive that experience."

Steve graciously offered his tent to Nina but she shivered in the chill of the desert night saying, "But I'm afraid and I don't want to be alone." So they both entered Steve's tent and lay down on the wide-open sleeping bag that was just a bit too warm.

Nina huddled in Steve's arms still shaking from her fright. Steve could feel the taut nipples of her warm untethered breasts against his chest as he struggled for a control that just wouldn't come. Despite his efforts, his now erect penis was pressed against Nina's thigh and she was more than aware of its presence. She reached down as she turned towards Steve and placed his penis close to her crotch. This didn't help a bit nor did Nina's warm kiss on his mouth as she murmured her thanks for his prompt action in saving her from the deadly Mamba. It took but a shake for Nina to shed her nightgown and pull Steve's shorts off. Then she knelt astride him as if she were a proud horsewoman with her back arched and her hands on Steve's thighs. Her fulsome breasts swung gently as she rose and settled down in synchronous movements with Steve's thrusts. Her turgid nipples were like rigid coral cones.

They clutched each other tighter and tighter as their hands began a caressing exploration of one another. Steve gently fondled her and felt the dewey lips of her mount. Nina guided his tumescence to enter as she turned over and rolled Steve atop her panting body.

He was full and harder then he had ever been before and penetrated deeply as Nina arched her back and pulled his buttocks towards her. She screamed, shuddered and shuddered again and again as they moved in unison towards a resounding climax, not just once but again and again.

Nina flew from crest to crest as her spirit soared into the night coming back only to repeat the startling flight of mounting surges. When they finally parted both were hot and panting in the stillness of the moonlit Kalahari night. Things would never be the same for them again.

Not a word of endearment passed between Steve and Nina, but yet each knew that a solid commitment had been made and that they belonged to one another. The next few days were idyllic. Perhaps not enough attention was given to the object of their trek, but they made up for it with the attentions they paid one another. This was a honeymoon that was lasting!

Finally, having searched and explored one another to the utmost, there came a time of waning of their awesome passion. Their thoughts slowly returned to their reason for being in the wide dry expanses of the Kalahari desert.

They were able to set up and break camp a bit more quickly now that only one tent was being used. The full moon was waning in the cool Kalahari night as Steve and Nina held each other close.

Krkchk and other members of his small band had seen the Land Rover now for several days. He and his fellow Bushmen knew that they had not been seen as their skill at concealment was outstanding. The Bushmen had no designs on the intruders into their land. They were merely curious and speculated that the invaders might be friendly and have food to offer. Still they harbored unspoken concerns that urged them to approach the vehicle and its occupants under cover of darkness and at a time when their owners might be least prepared for a visit by the Bushmen.

Krkchk and Kirkl chatted briefly about how they might best approach the Land Rover and the campers. Their speech was oddly different from most other languages of the world as they chatted in the San dialect of Khoisan, one of the few "click" languages.

Krkchk and Kirkl could have been brothers so alike they were in size and appearance. They were each about 4 ft.2 in. tall. Their small rounded heads were wrapped in tattered rags mainly to keep the sweat out of their eyes. The only other clothing they wore were pieces of antelope skins around their thighs. Little more than a G string, the antelope skins were not worn for modesty, but mainly to protect tender genitalia from the thorny bushes that were encountered all too frequently in the barren Kalahari desert.

What hair they had was short and tightly kinked. Their tawny eyes were in deep sockets surrounded by crinkly folds that protected them from the harsh rays of the brightly burning sun. Their chests were bare. Tautly muscled arms carried a few bands of copper that served as ornamentation, although now and then a sharp sliver of rock or thorn would be held there for future use.

Their protruding butts stored fat and seemed to give the short huntsmen a weighted balance not granted to other people. The larger the bottom on their women, their greater appeal to the men of the tribe.

Their legs were well muscled and any Bushman could trot the day long over the desert pausing only to grab a lizard for lunch or to relieve himself when necessary.

When the tribe was on the move, the men slowed a bit and the women and children kept the pace. At times, the men left the tribe for days to hunt down the game on which their existence depended. Water was scarce but every Bushman and his family had a mental record of the few water seeps that existed. Even so. they could go for days without a drop passing their lips.

It had been almost four days since the lioness had last eaten. She was pregnant and the extra weight tired her as well as increased her hunger. It was particularly difficult to hunt in the wide open vastness of the Kalahari. Game was scarce as well. But the lioness and her pride had been residents of the desert as had her forefathers for generations. Hence, they eked out a meager existence on what the Kalahari had to offer. Now and then an antelope would fall to the hunter's skill. With almost equal certainty, the Bushmen themselves became a meal for the hungry pride.

The huge lioness stood on a low hill that overlooked the Land Rover camp. She sniffed and concluded there could be something there for her. She cautiously descended into the draw pausing frequently. Now another smell assailed her sensitive nostrils. Bushmen were on the prowl as well!

Krkchk and Kirkl were completely unaware of the lion as they approached the trekker's camp from the opposite direction. With knobkerries in hand, bows on their backs, the two Bushmen moved slowly pausing now and then as they moved forward. Intent on the Land Rover and the single tent, neither of the hunters had any idea that a lion was nearby.

The lioness launched herself into the air and landed on the hapless Kirkl. A blood-curdling scream broke the desert stillness as her jaws clamped tightly on Kirkl's body. A fraction of a second later Steve exploded from the tent .308 rifle in hand. He fired at the lion. Startled at the noise and the searing flame in her shoulder, it released Kirkl and fled to the protection of the nearby hills.

Steve and Nina did what they could do save Kirkl as Krkchk stood by in shock at the rapid and awesome turn of events. Nina had the presence of mind to save some of the blood dripping from Kirkl's side. Their first aid kit was useful. Finally the bleeding stopped. Kirkl rested the remainder of the night as Nina, Steve and the frightened Krkchk did what they could to make Kirkl comfortable. Steve and Nina noted that the tiny Bushmen had tremendous stamina. By dawn Kirkl took the proffered bowl of soup and lapped it up voraciously.

Communications were difficult and only through signs and actions were Krkchk and Kirkl aware that the trekkers were friendly. That afternoon the Bushmen took off laden with gifts of food, cloth and implements that Steve and Nina had brought along to encourage the Bushmen to provide a blood sample. Now they had their sample although they had hoped to get one by some other means that would not have been so violent.

Steve and Nina followed the Bushmen slowly in the Land Rover. A few miles deeper into the Kalahari, they arrived at the simple camp consisting of about five families with a total of some twenty souls. The group was spread out in an ancient dry stream bed. Sticks and skins provided some shelter from the sun when in mid day the temperature soared to 120 degrees. There were signs everywhere of the brushfire that the Bushmen had set to burn down the scatterred grasses and make it easier for them to find and collect the bauhinia nuts that were an important staple of their diet.

"We can't stay here long or our sample may suffer, Steve. Let's give these people what food we can spare and the trinkets that we no longer need."

"Good idea!" and suiting action to the word they quickly passed out the food and goodies to the people surrounding the Land Rover.

The Bushmen were a sad lot! Wearing nothing but breech clouts while the children were completely nude, the entire group appeared ill nourished and dried out. Yet this was a normal existence for them-a continuous battle for existence in one of the world's harshest environments.

They wasted no time in retracing their outward bound route as they returned to Gabarone. The first order of business was to dispatch the sample to Alan at Denver University. The US Consul was especially helpful by sending the sample out in the diplomatic pouch.

With their mission accomplished Steve and Nina took stock of their situation. They loved one another and agreed that marriage should be the first order of business. Here too the Consul was helpful. Although there was no conventional way for the lovers to marry, there was a Zulu chieftain who had tribal authority to perform marriages. But, by custom, the Zulu had to receive a "bride price" from each couple he spliced. It turned out that this "bride price" was a heavy twisted bar of one inch square copper inscribed with ancient hieroglyphics. This was the principal source of the Zulu chieftain's wealth. Finding a "bride price" wasn't too difficult and Steve was able to locate one in the Gabarone bazaar. It weighed about five pounds and cost $50, close to the average annual wage of a Botswana worker. But Steve wasn't one to argue over price and planked down the money willingly.

After giving the "bride price" to the impressive Zulu headman, Steve and Nina were subjected to the marriage ceremony. They were shouted at and sung over as the Zulu chief and his warriors danced and chanted as they formalized the union of Steve and Nina. A well-decorated rondavel was provided and Steve and Nina were herded into it to consummate their marriage.

They stayed in the hut until dawn as they consummated. The Consul provided a document affirming that the marriage had taken place in complete accord with the customs of Botswana.

What next, thought Mr. and Mrs. Steve Pringle as they headed south to Johannesburg? There they turned in their rented Land Rover and make arrangements to ship their gear. They had only used up two weeks of their leave time.

"Look, honey," said Steve, "while we're in Africa it seems prudent to get a sample of Pygmy blood. We'll be real close to the tribe that lives in the rain forest of Gabon. Instead of just flying over them, what do you think about making arrangements for extending our stay and we can hunt up some Pygmies. After all it is our honeymoon."

There were other Pygmy tribes such as those that inhabited the Ituri rain forest of Zaire, but it seemed to Steve that the Pygmies of Gabon might be more accessible.

Nina mulled the proposal briefly and said, "Great idea! I'll call Alan and see if he'll give me a bit more leave."

"And I'll have to call the mine and make similar arrangements. I really don't think there will be any problem." He was right.

They made the calls from Johannesburg.

"Hello, Alan. This is Steve"

"Where in the world are you?"

"We're in Jo'burg, South Africa and having a great time. Did you get the blood samples we sent on via diplomatic pouch?"

"Yes, the sample came through in great shape and we've already begun work on it. Is Nina with you? I'd like to talk to her."

"Sure thing, Alan. I'll put Mrs. Pringle on."

"What did you say? Mrs. Pringle! So you guys had to go and get hitched? I should have known better than to leave you two alone. Well, put her on."

"Hi, Alan. Yes I'm Mrs. Pringle now and we are soooo happy. Will tell you all about it when we get home. But right now I should like to have permission to extend our stay a bit as we'd like to come home via Gabon and go to the interior and try to get some Pygmy blood samples."

"Sure, Nina, go ahead and get your samples. And, say, enjoy your honeymoon. I don't know what Mary is going to say about all this. You'll just have to make peace with her when you get here."

"Thanks, Alan. We'll do our best!"

Steve just had to have a busman's holiday and made plans to visit the Vaal Reef mine. Nina had ideas of her own.

"Steve, darling, that's a great idea and I want to go underground with you. I've never been in a mine and wouldn't want to miss this opportunity to go into one that's almost two miles deep. Besides, the mine trip will give us another unique opportunity to renew our vows - two miles down but with a real minister this time."

When Steve approached the mine manager with this idea, he found that the South African engineer thought the idea was a real blast and offered to serve as a witness to the ceremony.

It took several days to make arrangements and soon the group stood in a stope deep in the reef with the minister, the mine manager, the stope superintendent and four Zulu miners as witnesses to the unusual event. The Zulus didn't get to kiss the bride but gravely shook hands with the bride and groom. Each miner mumbled something in his native tongue that the stope superintendent translated as good wishes and many babies.

Then the venture was back on track again as Steve and Nina made plans for a flight to Libreville, capital of Gabon, the jumping off place to seek out a Pygmy tribe.

While Nina was readying their gear for the trip to Gabon, Steve went to a travel agency to arrange the trip. It took an hour and a half of plotting to get tickets to Gabon.

"There's no such thing as a direct flight. We gotta' go all around O'Hoolihan's outhouse to get to Libreville. We fly via African West Coast, known locally as AWC or Auk even though that flightless bird is thousands of miles away in the Arctic. First we go southwest to Capetown. then north to Windhoek in Namibia and on to Luanda in Angola. Then it's on to Ndolo airport in Kinshasa. There's a two hour layover in Zaire while they service our Auk. Then we cross the Congo river for a brief stop in Brazzaville at the Maya Maya airport and finally we land at Libreville."

Arrangements were made with Alan Muster to send another blood sample kit to Libreville. Actually the Pygmy tribe in Gabon was within a few hundred miles of Libreville. Few problems were anticipated. Arriving Libreville, the pair went through customs and checked in with the US Consul and explained their mission.

"What we're here for is to collect some samples of Pygmy blood."

Anticipating the Consul's questions, Steve went on to explain. "We are studying the makeup of the blood of various peoples to determine what makes them as they are."

Both Steve and Nina felt that it would be a significant mistake to reveal the real reason for the samples. It was better left unsaid. Fortunately the Consul was satisfied and agreed to help out.

Arrangements were made to ship the sought-for sample in the diplomatic pouch. The Embassy staff proved helpful in finding a guide for the expedition and an interpreter as well. This time Steve made no advance payments. These two would meet Steve and Nina in Lastoursville. With French the official language, Steve and Nina felt comfortable as they both had a smattering of high-school French

Gabon was malaria country and both had to have medication as well as shots for yellow fever and cholera. It was a bit different from the arid Kalahari. Here everything was dense jungle with all kinds of bugs, snakes and critters of all kinds. Even the pygmy elephant was found in the tropical rain forest And it rained almost every day.

Getting to the Pygmy area proved somewhat involved. First they had to travel by coastal steamer to Port Genteel. Then they had to charter a riverboat that would take them up the Ogooue River past Lambarene to a landing at Lastoursville east of the Chaillu Mts. Then they had to travel in a westerly direction until they ran across a Pygmy tribe. It was far more complicated than the search for Bushmen.

Lambarene was a city of some 60,000 located at the confluence of the Ogooue and Mgounie rivers. Steve and Nina stood by to see their gear unloaded from the ferry during the almost constant rain. They hired three boys to watch over the gear while they pursued arrangements for the trip up the Ogooue.

Nina told the boys, "We'll give you three francs each for guarding our gear and it will only be for an hour or so." The boys smiled with delight at the assignment and the high rate of pay. Nina and Steve had no problem in renting a launch that would take them up the hundred miles of Ogooue and wait for them until they came back to Lastoursville for the return trip to Lambarene. The 26 ft. long launch was operated by a crew of three including the skipper-owner. They were all about the same height and age. Steve found it difficult to tell them apart. Nina was more observant and noted slight differences so she could distinguish the French-speaking crew members of the Mpongwe tribe.

Dollars were exchanged for francs at the rate of 252 per dollar. Provisions, mainly canned goods, were purchased along with other supplies. They had their weapons and ammunition and most important, the blood sample bottle in its dry ice container. Local arrangements were concluded for air pickup of the sample from the US embassy at Libreville.

A two day search resulted in Steve finally locating a Cessna that would pick them up when they were ready to depart. It was far from a comforting sight. Steve noted the peeling paint, the pock-marked prop and the broken door latch replaced by a rubber band cut from an inner tube.

"Will this thing fly? We have to be sure as the stuff we get in the bush has to get to the US Consul as quickly as possible."

"Not to worry." said the pilot, a displaced West Virginian who looked like a Gabon native. "I been flying this bird for four years. She may not look like much but her engine is in great shape. The flight from Lastoursville to Libreville will be done in jig time with only an hour from the time you hand me the sample 'till delivery. Take this single-side-band radio and give me a buzz when you got your sample ready to be picked up."

By most standards the people of Gabon were far better off than those of the other central African nations. Petroleum, uranium, manganese and timber exports contributed to the $3,750 average annual income which was more than ten times that of neighboring Equatorial Guinea.

Steve and Nina were enjoying the sights, sounds and smells of their honeymoon but their surroundings on the launch were far from conducive to other aspects of a honeymoon. The limited space on the launch was no deterrent to the natives. They moved past Boo on the Equator where the north-flowing , tea-colored river took a turn to the west as it flowed on to the coast.

As the launch cruised slowly upstream, there were frequent visitations by dugouts from the settlements along the Ogooue river. Some dugout crews came to trade offering fresh fruits and vegetables. More often the dugouts brought lissome teenage girls to the launch for joyous couplings with the crew members at any time of the day or night and in full view of the passengers. Up river progress slowed when all three of the crew were so engaged. Steve and Nina were abashed by the uninhibited and athletic sexual activity being performed at their feet.

Having put down a boat crew, the girls took what francs were tendered and departed to their awaiting dugout and were ready for the next launch to arrive. These were the Gabonese distributors of AIDS, and whatever other sexually transmitted diseases that could be named. They were ever-ready females that didn't require any time to dress or undress as a less than six inch leather flap suspended by a waist thong was their sole attire.

It was understandable that the population of Gabon was expected to increase from 1.1 million in 1993 to 1.8 million by 2025. Here was a shining example of the need for smaller people with a lower sperm count. Steve was inclined to admire the sexual performance of the crew members who seemed able to have sex as many times a day as the opportunity was offered.

"Look," cried Nina as a group of hippos paddled lazily towards the launch. "What enormous creatures! Yet so mild and tame, as if they were just trying to be friendly."

"Don't you believe it. One of those buggers could take a bite out of a dugout and even kill it's crew if it wanted to." Just about then one of the huge hippos opened its mouth.

"Wow, I can understand that. Look at that mouth. It's as big as a suitcase. And those teeth are sized to match."

The launch skipper noted their interest in the hippopotami and in his halting French said, "Wonderful animals. Not tame, but yet not as vicious as crocodile. But if Madam doesn't keep from dabbling her fingers in river, she may find she has fewer to count if she doesn't lose an entire arm." This was warning enough and Nina abruptly ceased trailing her fingers in the brown waters of the Ogooue.

Each night the crew landed the launch near one of the many river settlements. Steve and Nina erected their tent and cooked up a meal while the crew members sought out whatever pleasures they might find nearby.

Three days out the current of the Ogooue increased and slowed the launch's speed. Finally the launch put in to a right-bank landing. A waiting shore crew hauled the flat-bottomed launch from the river on rollers. A harness was fastened to the bow and with ropes on both sides of the roller track, crews of Fang tribesman were able to haul the launch uphill .

Steve and Nina walked along with the crew members. Soon the reason for the land travel of the launch became apparent. A waterfall stretching across the river made boat passage upstream impossible. Native ingenuity had overcome the problem with the roller track.

Back on the Ogooue again, it only took part of a day to reach Lastoursville. Their guide and the interpreter were waiting. Cargo carriers were hired to handle the food and water, tents and the other gear. They finally got started with the guide in the lead. The interpreter came next followed by Steve and Nina with the 12 cargo carriers bringing up the rear. The various bundles and boxes were carried on their woolly heads.

The tropical heat was intensified by the enervating high humidity. It rained almost constantly. Everything smelled of rot. Plant life grew rapidly, and died quickly too. Leeches and bugs of all kinds were abundant. Steve and Nina wore their headnets that only seemed to stifle them more in the damp still of the jungle. Their guide followed a track that was almost invisible to Steve.

Both were exhausted when the interpreter finally said it was time to make camp. With swinging machetes, all joined in the working of making a clearing about 30 feet square in the dense jungle. All the brush was cut down to ground level but big trees were spared. This scar was a most temporary thing. Everything grew so rapidly that the clearing would disappear in a few weeks.

During the night, they heard the distant yodeling of the rain forest Pygmies. Together with the Swiss, they were the only peoples known to practice this unusual type of singing where the voice fluctuates from a normal chest voice to a falsetto. The unexpected medley of the Pygmies in the still of the deep tropical night was interrupted by various animal sounds.

Three days into the jungle, they were discovered by a small band of Pygmies. Their guide had sensed that the expedition was being followed and observed. But it was only when they had all entered a clearing that the travelers found themselves looking into the bent bows of some almost nude diminutive warriors. This was the time to be grateful to the interpreter. Before long his words of friendship put the Pygmies at ease and the bent bows were relaxed.

Signaled to follow, the group went off into the jungle at a sharp angle to their route of travel and soon came to the Pygmie's village. Both Steve and Nina thought that the jungle had smelled but they were unprepared for the clean and fragrant Pygmy village. Dogs roamed among the Pygmies as well as their tiny offspring. Clothing was evident only now and then. The women were busy with cooking fires and making the nets that each Pygmy male carried on the hunt. These people were true hunter-gatherers that lived in harmony with their forest home.

Nina and Steve and the interpreter were led before a Pygmy who was close to four feet tall. In addition to a breech clout he wore a decorative head dress that distinguished him from his followers. Through the interpreter Steve explained their reason for intruding on the Pygmy domain. His story wasn't quite true.

"Great Chief, we come to you as supplicants. There are people in other tribes who suffer greatly. Their seers and wise men. say that only a rare ingredient found in the blood of the Pygmy tribe can cure the disease. Not much would be needed, Steve explained, but we hope that your eminence will see fit to grant this request that would be so helpful to the ailing tribe."

The Chief replied,"That is really no problem. We frequently bleed our warriors as a preventive measure to protect them from ills that might otherwise affect them and you may have your sample."

The Chief went on to say, "A small exchange will be needed. The blood sample is a trifling matter, but I will add fifteen goats and a tame monkey and you, in exchange, will give me the white woman who will join my other wives in making me happy."

"What a dilemma," thought Steve., but he said to the Chief, "That would be a great honor for the white woman, my wife, but from my experience she is worth far more than fifteen goats, maybe as many as thirty!" a number that Steve had observed exceeded the goat population of the village. A well-placed kick in the shins and a muttered, "You bastard!" expressed Nina's view of the turn of events.

The bargaining went on for some time, but the alternate gifts proposed by Steve plus Nina's shrewish behavior was convincing. It was apparent that the Chief sought compliant women and not a white giant that might best him in any struggle.

Turning towards her ear Steve whispered "We may be missing a bet. What if the 'smaller' genes we seek are only in a woman's blood? I think we should try to get another sample. If you ask and do it right, that old reprobate wouldn't turn you down." She nodded her agreement and signaled to the interpreter that she wanted a word with the diminutive chief.

"Great leader, you have highly honored me by your request. I regret that it cannot be. But we must reward you for tendering me what would be a real privilege, the opportunity to share with your other wives the glory of being ever by your side. We wish you to remember us kindly and want you to have this gift of ten thousand francs. But we have one further request, oh mighty one, to render aid to the ailing women of our tribe, may we have a sample of the blood of one of your fortunate wives?"

Sagely the Chief slowly nodded his head while he thought "Now I'm in luck. With such a sum I could buy a number of new wives, Yes, even a shotgun to use in the hunt. And now I can get rid of that troublesome one as well." He murmured something to one of his warriors, who smiled and left the gathering. In a few minutes he was back with a shy teen-aged girl who kept trying to wriggle from the warrior's grasp.

"Your gift is welcome and I accept this in remembrance of your visit. But you also shall have a memento of your trip to our village."

He waved towards the now angry girl. "Shala is yours! She has much blood for sample."

This wasn't quite the turn of events that the intruders sought. What in the world would they do with this surly child? Stunned as they were, they saw no way to escape from this bind and accepted the Chief's largess. Later, they would have to figure a way to get a sample of Shala's blood and get her back to her tribe.

Soon after the group resumed it's return journey Shala succeeded in breaking loose from her captors but was quickly recaptured.

Fortunately, during her truggles to escape, Shala scratched her arm on a thorny bush. Nina took over and dressed the wound but only after capturing a sample of Shala's dripping wound. Now they could rid themselves of this tiny troublemaker. It was only necessary to leave Shala unguarded for a moment and the lithe girl vanished into the dense forest.

The group made a forced march through the rain-drenched forest to Lastoursville where Steve radioed for the Cessna float plane to come and pick them up. Arrangements were made to handle their gear and pay off several obligations. Two hours later they were in the US Embassy in Libreville and the blood samples were dispatched to Alan's laboratory in Denver.

The next day Steve and Nina flew on to London to rest up a day or so at the Grosvenor hotel before returning to Denver. At least it was their intent to rest but their interrupted honeymoon was resumed after a few hours rest. They spent the two days enjoying each other with rapture. But then it was their flight day. The pair were met by Alan and Mary Muster at the Denver International airport.

The blood samples from the Bushmen and the male and female Pygmies had arrived in perfect shape and work was already in progress to determine what genes were responsible for the various characteristics of the two types. They knew that it could be helpful to have some blood from the Pygmies of Luzon in the Philippines, but that could wait as there was plenty of work to be done on the samples from Africa.

CHAPTER 4.
THE PLAN

It was no surprise to the Musters that Nina and Steve had become Mr. and Mrs. Pringle. The newlyweds were living in Steve's home in Evergreen. Once settled in and rested up from the ardors of their African adventure, they invited Alan and Mary to celebrate their marriage and homecoming. But Mary was full of questions.

"How did this happen? You were supposed to be a working team and not get into any fiddle-faddle. When did you decide to get hitched and where? Are you really married or just planning to set up light housekeeping. Show me some proof or I'm gonna' insist that you have a real wedding here. I don't think you were fair to include us out in the first place!"

The Zulu document was ample evidence and Steve fortified the story of their bonds with the recounting of the ceremony held almost two miles deep on the Rand. Mary, in particular, felt cheated that she had not participated in the pairs union. Her feelings about the need for a repeat wedding were considered, but Mary was finally prevailed upon to put her idea on ice. There were other things that needed doing.

Laboratory workers under the direction of Alan and Nina were busy in a concerted effort to take the measure of the genes of the African samples. They sought the specific places of the genetic codes that could be tagged and single DNA molecules fished out for recombination. This was a monstrous task.! With some 100,000 genes, plus or minus 50,000, there was a mountain of exploration work in progress. This monumental effort was going to take money-lots of it.

So far, Denver University had listened to Alan's pleas and funded the sample collecting and the lab work. But now, as they looked ahead, it seemed evident that the university was unlikely to be able to fund the massive tasks that lay ahead.

They did know where they were going, but the path was torturous and uncertain. Alan and Nina with the collaboration of Steve debated the concept.

"What we are after," said Steve, "is people that are smaller. They shouldn't be over four feet tall. We want these future inhabitants of the earth to have a lower sperm count than applies today. If possible, we want to eliminate or reduce the greed factor."

Alan shook his head and allowed, "That's a big order, but should be attainable-at least in theory."

"Suppose you are successful, what then?" Mary, ever practical, asked. "So you have the means to create this new race. Then what? Will you set up clinics where everyone can come in and get an injection so their offspring will be endowed with all these new qualities? Some will go for it, but you'll never get the majority to take those shots. The world will end up with a deadly mix of what we call normal people like those of today and the midgets. There'll be conflicts the like of which you've never heard tell of."

"I think you're right! But we have to find a way. If we don't, then all we have done to date is find an answer to which there is no question." exclaimed Steve.

When the group went their ways at the end of the evening, there was a consensus that they should each think about the problem and, hopefully generate some useful ideas that they could toss around at their next get together. In the meantime, the laboratory work had some direction.

Stretches of genes were sought that could be transplanted into humans so that their chromosomes would be passed on to the next generation. Thousand of hours of laboratory work, tens of thousands of petri plates, tons of yeast had to be expended as the research teams groped for the answer. The hum of nearly fifty centrifuges was near constant.

Nina played a key role in staffing the laboratory and in seeing that consistent procedures were followed in examing the samples and their clones in seeking out those certain genes that affected height. Weeks were spent in interviewing candidates until both Nina and Alan felt that they had engaged sufficient numbers of scientists and researchers to do the job ahead.

Steve stayed close to this procedure and expressed his curiosity about where the work was going. Nina tried to keep him informed.

"You've got to understand, Steve, that there is going to be a lot of hit and miss in this effort as the principle that genes controlling different traits are inherited independently of one another turns out to true only when the genes occur on different chromosomes. Genesare arranged on the chromosomes in a linear fashion. It is only when the genes occur on the same chromosome that they are inherited as a single unit for as long as the chromosome itself remains intact."

"This linkage of genes is rarely complete. The combinations of alleles characteristic of each parent can get reassorted in some of their offspring. In the meiosis process, a pair of homologous chromosomes may exchange material or involve in recombination or cross-overs."

"How can these various situations you describe be determined?"asked Steve. "It isn't as if you could observe this like it was on a computer screen."

"That is exactly what it is. Those expensive microscopes we bought are designed to project the image of the view on the screen so more than one person may examine the image. There we see the X-shaped joint between two chromosomes -the effect of crossing over. What is more the screen will show how crossovers occur more or less at random along the length of the chromosomes. The frequency of recombination between two genes hinges on their distance from one another on the chromosome.

"But there is more to it, Steve. If the genes are relatively far apart, recombinant gametes will be common. If they are relatively close, recombinant genes will be rare. In the offspring produced by the gametes, the crossovers will show up as new combinations of visible traits.The more crossovers that occur, the greater the percentage of offspring that show the new combinations. Accordingly, we can arrange suitable breeding experiments. and plot the relative positions of the genes along the chromosomes.

That is why we will have these mice with their short gestation period. When they breed we can examine their blood under magnifications up to 400,000 times to see what has happened. When we change their genes and do it to the right ones, we'll be able to match the genes that make the pygmys small."

Molecular biology held no easy answers but due to a process that enabled reproduction of millions of cloned segments of DNA within hours, the seekers were reassured that their efforts had a chance to be successful. But there was a need for lots of money to continue the work-more than was available from Denver University.

Now and then Steve and Nina spent a restful weekend at their cabin north of Empire. Frequently they used the cabin as a base for further fishing and camping expeditions. For a long time Steve had forgotten the old drift that had been exposed by the rock fall so long ago.Their travels and sample collecting, the research for a recombinant DNA that would lead to the results they sought had absorbed all their time and energies.

Now, they sat on the cabin porch and watched the summer evening fade. "Honey. we've come a long way. The lab work you've been doing looks good and from what you and Alan tell me we are really on the track to come up with an injectable that will result in smaller children. At the same time, it looks like we're going to face some rough financial problems."

"I know and I don't have a clue what can be done about it. But we aren't up here to resolve the lab's problems. We're supposed to be resting and refreshing our minds. Then maybe next week this rest will help us to come up with an answer!"

As they sat on the cabin porch their attention was again directed to the mysterious opening high up on the cliff face. They needed a diversion and perhaps this was it. They chatted more about how to get in to the old drift.

"I can't stand it any more. That old hole in the cliff has been bugging me for years. I've got to get into it one way or another!"

"That's OK. I can understand how you feel. But please be careful. You know I love you and I don't want to have anything happen to you 'specially since we've had so little time together. You will be extra careful, won't you?"

"Sure, I'll be careful. I don't want to end up with a broken neck or anything else. I've got to love you lots more and then there's the job in the lab."

The next morning Steve got out a back pack and began to pack the items he would need for exploring the old drift-a geology pick and sample bags, water, a snack, a carbide lamp and some extra miners lump. He gathered up enough rope to reach from the cliff top to the bottom.

Steve climbed an old trail up the valley. When he thought he had gotten above the elevation of the cliff top, he began to climb out of the valley. Working his way through the pines, he began to see more light as he approached the edge of the cliff. They could see each other as Steve emerged from the pines.

Nina waved him over to a point directly above the old mine opening. Steve secured his rope to a large Engelman spruce that lay about twenty feet back from the cliff face. Carefully, he let the rope down until it was fully extended with the loose end resting on rubble at the foot of the cliff. Then he tied his pack to the rope end and lowered it to the base of the cliff.

He passed the rope under one thigh and over the opposite shoulder and cautiously rappelled down to the mine opening. He pulled the pack up and then worked his way into the drift for several feet before releasing the rope. With his lamp lit, Steve waved to Nina and began his exploration. He moved slowly as he observed the hand-cut timber sets placed by miners of at least a century and a half ago. From what he could see of the exposed rock, there was no mineralized structure that could have been of interest to the miners of time past.

About 200 feet along the opening he came to a point where a drift ran at an angle to his entryway. Looking up Steve could see the milk-white vein of quartz that was intercepted by the crosscut he had entered from the cliff face. This was what those old miners had been seeking! Steve took note that the drift ran in both directions from the intersection by the crosscut.

He marveled at the persistence of those old timers. Stacked nearby he saw many pieces of both dull and sharp hand steel. Length varied from a foot to a foot and a half. The 7/8ths inch hexagon steel was mushroomed at one end where it had been hammered on with a single jack. The working end was a single chisel bit. Looking between the skillfully installed timber sets, Steve could see the remnants of the hand-drilled holes that the miners had placed to achieve their advance.

It appeared that the blasting of each round placed had added about a foot of length to the drift.

For his initial exploration, Steve turned to the right. The quartz vein exposed here and there between the timber sets was about three to four feet in width. The dust of successive blasts made the quartz structure barely visible. Some 120 feet down the drift he was overcome with shock to see two figures seated upon a pile of precut timbers.

As he got closer he saw that the figures were the mummified remains of the men who had driven the openings. Their clothing was reasonably intact and their features were distinguishable. Stuck in a nearby set were two candleholders with about three inches of candle in each.

"What happened here?" thought Steve. He moved on some sixty feet to the end of the drift. There was a pile of broken muck from the last round the miners had detonated.. "What killed those guys?" he pondered. Getting closer to the face he saw that the last blast had exposed a vug, a cave-like void, in the vein. Crawling over the muck pile Steve held up his lamp for a better look and saw that the vug was the full width of the vein, about twenty feet long and fifteen feet or more in height. It was about eight feet wide. And what a sight!

The walls of the vug were studded with clear quartz crystals enlaced with wire and crystalline gold..This was the goal of the miners. It dawned on Steve what had killed those two. Gases trapped in the vug and released by the blast had wiped them out just as they found the riches they sought. Fate was unkind!

What to do? He was anxious to get back to Nina and tell her of his discovery but knew there were a few things he had to do first. He entered the vug and carefully pried loose a few of the beautifully formed crystals with their golden fittings. He wrapped the specimens in his bandanna and secured the packet in the pocket of his jacket. Then he returned to the cross-cut and took a quick look at the other end of the drift. The face was still in the quartz vein. Deftly he cut a chip sample across the width of the vein and placed the pieces in his other pocket. At least he had one sample to send for assay.

His examination of the ancient mine working had taken an hour and he knew that Nina would be concerned if he didn't show up soon. When he got back to daylight and looked down at the cabin, there stood Nina, waving. Steve waved back and then rappelled down the rope to the cliff base. Back at the cabin he showed his spectacular specimens to Nina. She was ecstatic over the beauty of the eight ounce clusters of gold-bound crystals. .

"Gosh, Steve, you sure were lucky to find such rare and lovely pieces, We can put one on the mantel and it will be a wonderful thing to show our friends!"

"Wait! Don't get carried away by these few chunks of lovely stuff!" He went on to explain the full extent of his find as Nina kept getting more and more excited.

"Now wait a minute. I want to tell you just what I saw when I went into the drift. The place where I went in was a crosscut that intercepted the vein. I turned to the right down the vein and got a gosh-awful scare. There were two men, or rather their mummified remains, seated on a few old mine timbers. At first, I couldn't figure out what killed them but when I saw the vug I finally realized that some kind of poisonous gas escaped from the vug at the time of the blast, floated down the drift and overcame the two miners. There was no warning, just rapid death for those two."

" My gosh, how awful for them! And just when they had stumbled on to great riches. I want to see it, I must see it. When can we have a look? "

"Steady now. You'll see it soon enough. But there are some things we must do first. Is all of the vein on our land?

Or do we have to buy some more? Then what do we do with the stuff.? This is specimen material that is worth far more than its gold content because of its sheer rarity and beauty. How are we going to extract the specimens so they won't be damaged? We have a lot of things to think about and plans to make."

"Vugs like this one are rare but can be phenomenal. I can remember one in particular that I read about that was found in the Cresson Mine at Cripple Creek in 1914. It was 14x23x36 feet and was blanketed completely with glittering crstals of sylvanite, calaverite and metallic gold. It took a month to cut out and sack the material into 2,500 numbered sample bags. When the job was finished, the Cresson Vug had yielded 60,000 ounces-a bit over two tons of gold worth $1.2 million."

"Wow! And to think that we may have something like that. This is overwhelming!"

"It sure is! We've got to take care of many things before news of this vug leaks. One of the first things we must do is to make sure that no adventurous soul gets into that old drift."

"How can we do that? It seems that anyone who wants to climb down a rope could get in without any problem."

"Yeah, and that is the problem. We need to close off that old crosscut in a way so that no one could get into the drift. We sure would have a heck of lot of problems if someone learns about our vug. We have to figure out some way to close the crosscut and still allow me to get in."

With a few days Steve had come up with several schemes to close off the crosscut in such a way as only he could have access. Most of the ideas were abandoned for one reason or another.

"Nina, I think I know how to close that crosscut. I'll lower about six pieces of mine drill steel down to the crosscut entry. I'll cut them about six feet long which is six inches or more longer than the heighth of the cross cut. Then I'll use some of the old pieces of short drill steel that I found in the drift and drill short holes into the back and the invert of the crosscut. I'll make these sets of up and down holes about 8 inches apart. That's close enough so that no grown person could squeeze through. Then I can stick a piece of steel into the up hole and then lower it into the lower hole. If I cut the holes properly, the steel will go into the lower hole with several inches still in the up hole. Later I'll grout in the permanent pieces of steel."

"That sounds pretty good, Steve, but how are you going to get in after you've cemented in all that drill steel?"

"I think I've got that figured out. I'll have some lugs of a piece of half inch steel two inches square welded onto two of the pieces of drill steel about 8 inches above the lower end. There'll be a three-quarter inch hole drilled in each lug. Then I'll have two short pieces of steel fitted with similar lugs welded to one end. I'll drill holes a few inches away from the loose pieces of drill steel and grout in the short drill steel. Then with a piece of chain and padlocks, I can close off the drift to any curious adventurer."

"Sounds like a lot of work to me. And you'll have to do it all alone. You're not going to get me into those old workings until you have a better way of doing it."

In Idaho Springs Steve found all the materials need to make his closure for the crosscut. In several days of hard work the job was done.

"I feel a lot better about our discovery now that we can keep it a secret and prevent thievery as well. Now we had better get on with the other things that need doing."

Steve dug out the maps and other data that were involved with his purchase of the Minnesota Mines claims. Along with the USGS topography sheet of the area, he was able to arrive at a fairly close siting of the old mine workings with respect to the claim boundaries. To his dismay, he found that the vug was just within his land but that the vein extended into neighboring claims. They just had to acquire the additional land to be sure they owned enough should other "jewelry store" vugs occur along the vein. They needed ownership anyhow for the vein itself could prove to be a profitable mine.

A check of the county records showed that the two claims were held by an absentee owner. Further checks with the office of the Clear Creek County recorder showed that no affidavits of assessment work had been filed for six years. Therefore the two claims of interest to Steve could be restaked and filed on in his name. The very next weekend he and Nina took to the hillside to re-stake the claims.

They laid out two claims, end to end, each 1500 feet long and 600 feet wide. They estimated the location of the concealed vein and put the claim sides at 300 feet to each side of where they thought the vein was. Location notices were placed on the corner stakes. Several stakes on each of the two claims were referenced to the summit of Red mountain and a peak due south of Empire. Brunton compass bearings were taken for relocation should the stakes be lost.

After recording the newly located claims at the Clear Creek County court house in Idaho Springs, they were ready to take the next step. They needed a way to gain access to the old drift that would be better than rappelling down the cliff face. Using his Brunton compass and counting paces, Steve made a map of the cross- cut from where it was cut off at the cliff face, into the intersection of the vein and the drift along the vein. Then he stood at the cliff edge and guided Nina to a point on the opposite side of the valley that was at the same elevation as the drift. She drove a stake at that spot. But what was the distance from the cliff face opening to the stake?

Steve figured out what he had to do and signaled Nina to walk along the valley side to another point at the same elevation as the cross-cut opening and, several hundred feet away, she drove another stake at the point Steve indicated would serve to solve the problem. Then he descended the cliff and rejoined Nina at their cabin. From a dusty corner closet he dug out his plane table and alidade. He set the plane table tripod over the second stake Nina had placed uphill from the cabin. After orienting the table with the instrument's compass, he had Nina hold a stadia rod on her first stake and established the distance from the plane table to that stake with the stadia cross hairs of the instrument.

The next step was to determine the distance to the cross-cut opening on the cliff. Nina took the rod to a point just below the mine opening on the vertical cliff face. Steve read the stadia and the vertical angle. Then he reduced the measurement to the horizontal distance and plotted it on the plane table. Now he had a map of the cross-cut in relation to the two stakes. When he plotted the mine workings on the plane table he could see the relationship of the mine drift to the stakes.

Projecting the strike of the vein, Steve picked a point on the valley's western side. Showing Nina his rough map, he said, "Look here, honey, if we drive a short cross-cut from here, we should intercept the vein."

"I think I understand, but what's that gonna' cost? We're short of money to meet the lab payroll and buy supplies."

"Wait till you see that vug. I think our money problems will be history once we get to that vug and can cut samples for sale. We should soon have more than enough money to cover all our expenses and, yes, even buy you that new four-wheel drive you want."

Now the cross-cut had to be driven. They contracted with a local miner to do the job A pioneer road was built to the portal site, a compressor set up and the cross-cut was driven by conventional drill and blast methods. At 165 ft. the cross-cut intercepted the vein. The material from the vein was pretty good by itself as it assayed 38 grams of gold per ton based on sampling the full width of the vein with thirteen cuts spaced three feet apart. But Steve was more interested in the spectacular specimens of the vug.

The contractor had begun drifting along the vein towards the end of the old drift that had encountered the vug of precious specimens. All of the vein material was stockpiled as its high grade gold content dictated that it be processed at some future date. As the drift progressed along the gold-rich vein, the distance to the surface increased. The material above the drift and that estimated by projecting the vein downward indicated that they had acquired the means whereby the Pringle Progression could be fully financed.

Most important to obtaining funds quickly was the specimen material of the vug. It was an unexpected and a pleasant surprise when the drift broke into another vug that was some 60 to 80 feet distant from the first vug intercepted in the old workings.

It appeared that they might have in hand the means to finance all the work that had to be done. There was no way to estimate what the specimens would sell for. Neither were there the funds to fully develop the vein and construct facilities for processing the ore. The quickest possible way of generating the cash for their research work seemed to be from the sale of the gold-quartz specimens Getting them out was a problem.

"We just can't drill and blast," Steve told the contractor. "Lots of the specimen material would be ruined."

Bob Mears, the Idaho Springs contractor, agreed. "I think I know how to do it. Years ago I worked at the Sweet Home mine, over by Alma. They mined specimen material-rhodochrosite. They wanted to get as much of the void walls as possible in the largest pieces possible and with the crystals intact. That ruled out blasting.

"They drilled a close pattern of horizontal holes only inches apart around the void. Then a hydraulic splitter served by a small air-driven hydraulic pump was used to break the vug walls along the line of the drill holes. They used a diamond chain saw to cut out big chunks of the vug walls."

"That seems to be the way we'll have to go." Steve allowed. "If it worked for them, it should work here just as well and we'll have some beautiful specimens to market."

A trip to Denver and visits to a number of supply houses resulted in the necessary equipment being on site within a few months. Steve and Nina impatiently awaited the specialized equipment that had to be put together. The very day it arrived, Steve put it to work and managed to cut out and carry outside the first salable specimen. It was about six inches square and had an overall height of six inches. Clear quartz crystals varying in height from one to three inches sprouted from the massive quartz base. Wire gold varying in diameter from a sixteenth of an inch to one eighth of an inch wound around the quartz crystals. First seen in daylight, the beauty of the specimen was awesome.

Nina marveled at the rare specimen and pondered, "What will such a thing bring on the market?"

"Who knows? The only was we'll find out is when we try to sell it to an appreciative buyer. Maybe we should try a Denver gem and mineral show and see what develops? There is a show coming up next month. Perhaps we could show three or four pieces?"

"I'll wear a low cut blouse and some tight fitting shorts. That ought to be bait enough to attract somebody. Then when we have gotten initial interest we can spring the specimens on them!"

There was no shortage of things to do. Mears constructed a reinforced concrete portal with a steel grate door that could be locked. It was fitted with an electronic signal so that if anyone attempted entry, the Sheriffs' office In Idaho Springs would know what was happening. A section of the outer wall of the vug was drilled and the hydraulic splitter, in combination with the diamond chain saw, resulted in the recovery of a number of striking samples. The recovered samples were stored in a huge safe that had been bolted down to a concrete slab in a corner of the cabin. By the time of the next Denver gem and mineral show they had six salable specimens ready to go.

They let the bidders set the prices on the six gold and quartz specimens. It came as a shock that the specimens sold for prices that ranged from $40,000 for the smallest to $100,000 for the largest.The six specimens netted $350,000. They were in business! Now there would be funds to build and equip a laboratory and really get moving on the progression towards smaller people and males with a lower sperm count.

An aggressive campaign at the mine produced more specimens. Soon they learned that the word of these unique sample had spread around the world.

"Gosh," Steve mused, "Things are going great. The news is traveling fast. Museums and gem dealers everywhere want our rare chunks of wire gold on quartz crystals."

"Too many specimens too soon would lower their market value. We can mine the samples at any rate, but we have to let them trickle on to the market in order to sustain their value." But there seemed to be no end to the demand. All the world knew that when the vug was mined out, there might not be any more of the rare and beautiful chunks. Steve and Nina were the only ones with the knowledge of the original vug and they kept that information to themselves.

At the next staff meeting Alan took the floor. "We have reached the point in our work where a change in direction is needed. We have a serum that we think will work. But that has to be proven and that means we have to move our efforts to the testing stage. The first step in that direction is the addition of a new wing that will be designed with cages and all the other stuff needed for animal testing."

Thinking outloud, Steve mused, "We want to do this right. Should have an architect with experience in designing animal facilities for research labs. We'll need whatever is called for to take care of up to five or six hundred mice, three or four hundred guinea pigs and perhaps space for a smaller number of larger animals. What we've got has to be demonstrated to do the job on a variety of animals before we can even think about launching human tests."

"Why so many mice cages?' asked Steve.

"Yeh, it does seem like a lot. But, remember,we will need space for holding mice still to be tested, cages for mice mating and then cages in which the active male mouse and the pregnant female mouse can be kept separate. Then the offspring will have to be kept separate from the full grown mice. It's gonna' take all those cages." Alan explained.

"And all the data on that army of mice will be computerized for record keeping?"

"That's right. It's no small task and we'll have to find an experienced computer operator to do the job."

An architect was found and engaged. There was no worry over finances as the gold-quartz specimens were selling and at prices Steve had never thought possible. "We've already sold five million two hundred thousand bucks worth of samples. The demand seems quite steady as more and more museums learn about the specimens. And we still have about 85 % of the material left in the first vug." Nina reported

She was so entranced with the sheer beauty of the jewelry-like vug that she wouldn't let anyone else handle the recovery and sale of the sparkling specimens.

In six months, but at extra cost, the new animal wing of the Golden laboratory was completed. Two hundred white mice were purchased first. Then the rigorous laboratory work began..

Centrifuges hummed, test tubes shook, dishes jostled and microscopes were peered into as some twenty researchers sought the "smaller" ingredient that would change people and the world. Numerous attempts ended in failure. It was a slow process. After each possible serum was generated, it had to be tested on lab mice.

Alan pointed out."There are four ways that mutations might be sought. One is to read the entire sequence of the gene and look for a "spellng" error. Another way is to use a probe that would chemically bind to the mutant sequence and "light up" to reveal it's presence. A third way is to place the DNA in a gelatin with a low voltage electric current running through it. Any mutation changes the electrical charge or shape of the DNA, and thus change the rate at which it moves through the gelatin in response to the current. A fourth method is to place the DNA in a protein synthesizer machine that "reads" the code contained in a gene and follows the instructions to make a protein just as a cell would do."

Sometimes the serums were fatal. There was always a wait to see the impact, if any, on the progeny of injected mice. For more than a year there was no sign of any success.

Steve was discouraged, although Nina tried to keep his spirits up. "This is the way research goes, honey. There are always more failures than anything else. Funds are no problem so we just have to hang in there and pray for both patience and success."

"I can understand that. But damn it, I want to see something come of all our work before the world comes apart from being over populated. There just has to be a way of attaining our objective. I cannot believe that the good Lord wanted mankind to follow the path of those many species that have vanished in those mass extinctions of the past. I believe that God designed a better future for mankind and I would hope that we can be his agents."

Alan did his best to temper Steves restiveness. "Hey, we're dealing with big, and I mean huge, monstrous numbers here. Within the DNA are some 250,000 genes, hence the numbers of combinations possible is astronomical. Each must be dealt with and tested to determine its effect."

Steve and Alan dreamed of their goals and felt certain they would have success in attaining them. It was difficult for all involved to keep their spirits high when failure upon failure was the order of the day. Some of the tests might be more promising. A core of eager scientists kept on plugging away seeking out the elusive genes on the DNA of the many chromosomes that were the key to the "smaller" people.

Each combination of genes had to be tested. Mice were used for this purpose and the tests had to be made with both male and female mice. It took several pairs for the conduct of each test. An untreated pair were mated as well as a pair where only the male was treated, where only the female was treated and a pair where both the male and female were injected.

Each pair was carefully weighed each day and subjected to rigid observation to detect any changes. When litters were born each mouse was carefully weighed daily and photographed for a record that might reveal significant changes.

Some strange things happened. Steve was in the lab every day and looked intently in every cage to see if he could see any changes. And one day he yelled, "Hey, Alan come look at this cage. It looks like these four mice are not normal. Look! Their hind legs are longer and bigger than their forelegs, Could these mice be the progenitors of a type that might have been the first critturs to walk on their hind legs?"

"Could be, Steve. We have to expect some weird results when we are messing around with the DNA of the mice"

The daily routine went on and on. Then one day one of the biologists that measured the changes in the mice called to Nina.

"Come here and take a look at this litter. They were born two weeks ago and already they are five times the size of other litters of the same age. We have had to transfer them to larger cages several times already."

"Gosh, I don't know. Maybe we had better get Alan and some of the others to talk about this before we do anything?"

"Wow," exclaimed Alan. "This is really strange. It just the opposite direction of the one we want to take. Let's get everybody together for a rump session to see what we should do about these little monsters."

Alan explained the accelerated growth rate of the seven mouse litter. "These mice are already big enough to take on any cat in the world and come out ahead. We have no idea where this test is going but it's 180 degrees from the direction we want to go. I would like to know how everybody feels about this particular litter."

The majority thought the test should be terminated. Several held the position expressed by Thomas Milton a very able microbiologist. "I know this is strange, but think what an opportunity we might have. If these tests were followed through, we might be able to create a race of supermen that could take over the world."

Steve interjected, "True, but that concept would bring about the destruction of the environment and mankind far sooner that if things were to proceed as they are now. I cannot and will not accept a course that deviates from our original objective."

Another vote was taken and there was unanimous agreement to terminate the test. Alan took charge of the termination phase of this unexpected development.

"I think we should use tranquilzer shots to put these giant mice to sleep. That will eliminate any problems that might arise in removing them from their cage. Once we have them tranquilized, we can take them outside and finish them off using my .22 rifle. Then that will be the end of what otherwise could be a serious problem of unknown dimension."

The tranquilizer shots did their job and the seven huge 20 pound mice went to sleep. Two had their lips curled back revealing their sharp teeth. The sleeping mice were carried out one by one to the yard in back of the lab. The first five were killed each with a single shot from the .22 rifle. But as Alan tured to shoot the two surviving giant mice they suddenly awoke and scurried into the woods at the rear end of the lab property.

"I doubt whether those mutant mice will be a problem." Alan conjectured. "They have always been fed and have had no parental training nor experience in hunting. Anyhow lets hope they'll just perish from natural causes."

"I sure hope it turns out like that. By the way, Alan, what sex were the escaped mice?"

" Gosh, I don't know. It doesn't make any difference as they aren't going to last long having to fend for themselves."

Several hours of searching for the escaped rodents failed to turn up anything. The search was abandoned at nighfall. On the next day a review of the records revealed that the the escapees were a male and a female.

"That makes the cheese more binding? We have to find those rascals and put them down. If we fail, we run the risk of having a litter of half dozen or more of the mutant mice to contend with in about ten weeks. We'll have to oganize a more thorough search for them tomorrow." urged Steve.

"You're right about that. What's more we don't dare let news of what has happened here leak out. The entire

Wimpfen

community would be upset and there would be pressures to close down the lab and end our research. I'm sure you don't want that to happen, Steve, so I think we should keep this problem in house. We should use our own staff to find those two even if we have to halt the research for the time needed to kill those mutant mice. "

"We can't shut down completely as the work in progress must be left in shape to permit its continuance later. Also the animals have to be cared for. Let's get the staff together and discuss this and the possible impacts. Then we can ask for volunteers. I'll buy about a dozen rifles in Denver. I'll get them from as many different gun shops to avoid arousing any suspicions."

Three days searching for the missing rodents failed to reveal a clue. Reports of missing pets and raids on hen houses were heard. Steve and Alan surmised the cause but kept quiet about their suspicions.

THE ROCKY MOUNTAIN NEWS
RETURN OF THE COYOTE ?
Golden, Colorado   October 10, 2012

Numerous reports have been received by local authorities of sightings of several coyotes with a particularly strange appearance. The large gray animals are said to stand about two feet high and are characterized by a sharply pointed muzzle and a long hairless tail.

It is thought that these furtive animals may be the cause of the dissappearance of many household pets in the area. Table Mountain is the scene of the majority of sightings. The Golden City Council has schedueled a special meeting to determine what action, if any, should be taken to correct the problems being caused by these strange animals.

"It's been a month since those damned giant mice escaped. Nothing has happened, at least not yet, to point to our lab as being the source of the problem. And we've got to be sure that nothing does. Hopefully the authorities will wipe out the critturs and our problem will be resolved. Is there anyone you may know on the Council that you can talk to about this, Alan?"

"I was thinking the same thing, Steve. There is a fellow named Parmel whom I can talk to."

Alan moved quickly to have lunch with Tom Parmel. This was something they did several times each year so Parmel was not surprised when Alan called.

"Hello, Tom. Haven't see you for some time. How about a few bottles of Coors and lunch?" A date was set and they met and chatted about the various topics that were of interest.

Finally Alan led the conversation around to the gray animals that were the source of the current pet problem.

"I understand from the papers, Tom, that the Council plans to do something about those strange coyotes that have been gobbling up all the pets of Golden?"

"That's right. We met last night and voted to hire four marksman to hunt the animals down. That should get the job done. But if, for any reason, that fails we are prepared to take more rigorous action. The people of Golden are upset about losing their pets. There is a concern that these strange coyotes could attack children. So we in the city council view this as a serious problem that must be resolved."

"I couldn't agree more." asserted Alan.

Two weeks later.

ROCKY MOUNTAIN NEWS
MYSTERY MICE DESTROYED
Golden, Colorado   October 24, 2012

After more than a month of having their pets disappear, the apparent cause of their demise has been eliminated.

100   Wimpfen

Marksmen employed by the Golden City Council found the animals near a cave on the south side of Table Mountain.

Examination of the bodies showed clearly that these were not coyotes nor even a variant of the coyote. They were clearly giant mice of unknown origin. Elimination of the pair was provident as the female of the species would soon have given birth to a litter of ten. This would have truly released a scourge on the community.

Scientists from facilities nearby and even from abroad have initiated a study of all data related to the giant mice in an effort to find out how they came to be.

Thousands upon thousands of DNA tests and genes combinations were conducted. Spirits rose and fell with the outcome of the many tests. Failure was the norm. But one, some 20 months after the search had begun, a single test resulted in a brood of mice that matured as far less than normal sized mice.

Parallel tests were made so the laboratory could then have several sets of the smaller mice that could, in turn, be mated to determine if their offspring would transmit the smaller genes to succesive generations of laboratory mice.

The tests upon mice were repeated using dogs and the success of the serum was proven when small Dobermans were produced in several generations.

"We need to know, not only that the 'smaller' serum works, but we also need to know what is the minimum amount that it will take to produce the results we want." postulated Alan. "If we can get by with just a few one hundredths of a millimeter of the serum, it will make the job easier."

This was a hectic time Ten pairs of mice were given half a millimeter injections. Then these treated mice were fed and weighed daily. Every bodily function was monitored and recorded. Computerized data could be easily tracked. But five days later all twenty of the mice had died.

"Something's wrong!" exclaimed Steve," But what?"

"This is a set-back, but that isn't unusual in this type of research. Actually, we are groping at this point. There are no criteria established to tell us what amounts to inject, so it's by trial and error that we have to move forward. We know we've exceeded that maximum of the serum that the mice can tolerate." Alan explained. "Now we have to back up and see if we can find the minimum amount of serum that will work."

Ten more pairs were injected with the serum, all with the tiniest droplet that could be formed using the finest needle possible.

The results were anxiously awaited. After the first ten days, it was a relief to find that all twenty of the mice were alive and well. When thirty days had passed each male was moved to a cage with a treated female. The mice were lively and quickly mated. Then the pair were separated again when it was apparent that the female was pregnant.

Finally the first litter appeared. The poor mouse was probably scared to death as her delivery process became the focus of attention as the researchers crowded around to see her first born. They were smaller by far than the newborn of untreated females. But the number in the litter was normal!

Steve and Alan were overjoyed to see the litter of ultra-tiny mice.

"Wow! This is what we dreamed of in those pre-mamba days in the Kalahari. Ya' know, I never thought of it before but that snake was a real match-maker. I'll be forever grateful to him."

The two couples went out on the town that night and toasted each other repeatedly for the success of their great undertaking that might change the world.

102

Repeated tests on mice confirmed the initial tests. The new-born mice of treated females were only half as big as mice from normal litters, but the number in a litter varied but little from that of untreated mothers. Further tests on rats and then with pigs proved to be consistent. Smaller sized creatures resulted when either one of the parents had been inoculated with the 'smaller' serum.

All this took lots of money. Fortunately the quartz-gold specimens sold well and more than $30,000,000 had been generated from the world wide sales of the unique crystals.

Although proven for animals it was a quantum leap to transfer the knowledge gained from mice and dogs to produce a serum that would work on humans. It was many months later that the biologists announced that they had developed humanoid serum that paralleled those used on mice and dogs.

Steve and Alan had a serum that was made up of genes that carried all the humanoid characteristics but that were modified to meet the goals established that provided for a people that were short–real short! Whether they had a lesser sperm count was not known. But if they did, it had to be sheer luck. When it came to the greed factor, it would take time and a different kind of research. What now?

"For one thing," said Nina, "We have to find out if the serum works. We must prove up the serum before we do anything else."

Nina was the brave one. "We have been involved in this from the beginning and I think that Steve and I should have the courage to take the next step." Steve agreed.

The very next day Steve and Nina drove to the lab determined to proceed with the injections of such historic promise. There was a small group present as Nina and Steve prepared to take the injections. The event was recorded on tape and still pictures so that posterity might learn about the momentous event. Now it was up to Steve and Nina to produce. They decided that a change, a kind of second honeymoon, might be in order to foster procreative circumstances. As the blood sample from the Philippine Pygmies still needed to be obtained it was agreed that the Orient was the place to go..

Northwest Airlines booked the pair into Manila via Anchorage and Tokyo. Instead of enduring the rigors of a straight -through trip Steve had a suggestion.

"Let's make this a real honeymoon. Let's stop off for a day or two in Anchorage and also in Tokyo. Then we won't be so tired when we reach Manila."

"That's a great idea! I think we should have a romantic candlelight dinner or two at each stop. That could help us to get the juices flowing as we look forward to our firstborn."

There had been no detectable side effects from their injections, a pleasant surprise to both. They had been prepared for some different sensations but there just weren't any.

The stop-overs in Anchorage and Tokyo and HongKong were idyllic, even though there wasn't much sightseeing. Most of the time was spent in lounging around their hotel quarters and enjoying each other in their concerted effort to miss no opportunity for the union of sperm and egg to create a baby. Never in history did any pair strive harder at the act of creation nor anticipate what their offspring might be. What's more, the baby they sought could play a most significant role in changing future history. Hence their arrival in Manila found them far from rested.

"Let's go shopping! We have to get stuff that will appeal to the Pygmies that might get them willing to let us take blood samples. I'm for some fancy knives and bolos."

"We have to get stuff for the women also." said Nina as she filled her bag with mirrors, beads and brass bracelets. "This should do it. Now lets get out of this heat and back to our air conditioned room for a while."

A few days in Manila were spent in gathering what gear they lacked for their trip north. They had with them most of the items used on their African venture.

Again, they rented a Land Rover as that vehicle had proven eminently dependable in Africa. Once loaded they took off for the north via San Fernando, Tarlac and Klondykes to eventually arrive at Baguio and the Pines Hotel. Steve found it hard to resist the impulse to visit a few of the notable gold mines in the area and finally caved in. Some of these deposits had been mined by the Chinese as far back as the time of the Ming Dynasty.

The mines continued to produce and looked forward to a long operating life under the free market for gold.

Several days were well spent in Baguio where Steve was unable to resist visiting a gold mine. He went south of Baguio to the famous Balatoc mine where he walked and climbed for four hours to grasp an idea of the geology, mineralogy and mining methods used. Steve's business card showing his association with the Henderson mine was a passport that opened every door.

Finally it was time to leave and travel the Mountain Trail to Bontoc. The Land Rover was loaded with everything they thought they might need plus extra gas and water. Two spare tires, already mounted on wheels, were strapped to the roof.

They headed out past the portals of Camp Holmes on a misty morning that was chilly and damp. The grandeur of the mountain ridges that formed the backbone of Luzon was soon apparent. The road that twisted and turned as it clung to a high ridge demanded constant attention. Now and then through a break in the clouds they could see many of the wedge-shaped mountains that lay to the east. Off to the west under the shroud of clouds was a broad patch of blue, the China Sea.

This precarious road was hewn from the mountains as a single car-width track. Gates were encountered frequently. There was usually a wait at a gate until a vehicle came through from the other direction carrying a crude flag signifying that the flag carrier was the last vehicle coming on the trail. Then they were allowed to go on carrying the flag to the north when they were the only car.

"Look, Steve, down there!" A break in the clouds showed bright green rice paddys at the bottom of a V-shaped canyon. These rice terraces were the life-blood of the various tribes that occupied the Mountain Province.

"Now I can understand why a tribe in one valley often had a different language and customs than a tribe dwelling in the next valley. There just wasn't any communication as travel was too difficult."

"Look, Nina! See that mountain off to the northeast. Watch the cloud cover and now and then in a break you can see Mt. Pulog. At 10,000 ft. that's the highest peak on Luzon."

"Don't these sweaters feel good? I had no idea we would ever need them ."

"It is cold, and with good reason. See the sign. This is Cot Cot Aso which is close to Mt. Data. We're up about 7,000 ft. above sea level and that's chilly even in the tropics." The many pine trees looked like conical apparitions as the fog swirled around them.

At every stop men and women clustered around the Land Rover in curiosity. Despite the chill the women young and old, wore only their tapis or woven skirts leaving them bare from the waist up. The men all carried the customary bolo and a few carried spears. Steve offered them gifts of trinkets, matches and soap. The people seemed to like the soap particularly as they ate it with relish.

They drove on past another gate where the road had been blasted out of a cliff face for some 400 feet. Then the road descended and finally they were below the clouds.

"Look, there is Bontoc. See there are some real buildings. One of them just has to a place we can spend the night."

They drove up to the Mountain View Hotel. A group of Bontoc boys grabbed their bags and led them to what passed for a lobby. They showed passports, signed the register and followed the clerk to a room. The boys were offered cigarettes but demanded centavos as a fee for their service. Steve was glad to pay them off and relax.

After a night in Bontoc, they proceeded north to Lubuagan and Balbalasang. There it was necessary to leave the vehicle and proceed on foot in their search for a Pygmy tribe. Local inquiries revealed that now and then a Pygmy would wander into the village, but for the most part the Pygmies were reported to be forest wanderers who kept to themselves.

It was up to Steve and Nina to find their quarry in the dense rain forest. It was a formidable task. "How in the world are we ever going to find Pygmies," Nina exclaimed, "when we don't have the foggiest idea where they might be between here and Kabugao?"

"Guess we'll just have to rely on dumb luck and hope for the best. One thing for sure, we had better get together a crew of Igorots who have some knowledge of the region and who are willing to see the effort through to the end."

That task took a few days. The Kalinga Igorots were busy with their daily lives but some were persuaded to join the search by the generous rate of pay Steve offered. Twelve men agreed to serve Steve which was just about what he wanted. Most of them had a smattering of English and the tallest man, named Tello Moclo, did pretty well.

They were a fierce looking bunch. On their heads they wore hand-woven round baskets about 7 in. in diameter and about 3 in. deep adorned with pig tusks. They ranged in height from 5' 6" to 5'10 "tall. Their attire consisted of a colorful hand-woven gee string about five inches wide that was wrapped around their hips so that a ten inch flap hung down in front and back.

Each carried a long fighting bolo and a few carried spears and shields. All were tatooed in one way or another. Except for one, who wore a pair of tattered once-white sneakers, all were barefoot. Each carried a small decorative basket that hung from the shoulder or on the hip to carry betel nut and lime.

"Steve, look at those two over there. They have several little V's tattooed on their lower jaws. Do those tattoos have any special meaning?"

"They sure do. No Igorot is entitled to have a V tattooed on his jaw unless he has taken a head. As far back in time as one knows these people were head hunters. Although the central government of the islands forbids this practice, it is like so many laws, completely unenforceable. In fact it still isn't safe for lowlander Filipinos to get off the beaten track in the Mountain Province for they may not be seen again."

Steve picked Moclo to be the leader of the group. The first thing to do was acquire supplies-food and whatever other things might be needed while they pursued the Pygmies in the dense forests of northern Luzon.

Moclo and the others disappeared for the rest of that day and finally reappeared carrying cases of canned pilchards and bags of rice wrapped in plastic. These loads were carried on their heads with their basket-like caps thrown back and left hanging from a cord that went around their necks.

" We have enough sor, for all of us to eat for two weeks.

If we get caught for longer time, must live off the land. You eat what we eat or go get special foods you think needed." Moclo commented.

"No need for special food. My wife and I can eat what you eat. Besides there is no use in burdening us down with extra loads. It seems to me that what we need to do is to cover as much ground as can and as fast as we can until we locate some Pygmies."

"That is right, sor, and to do that we only have six men to carry loads. Other six need cut trail so we can move."

The loads were distributed. They were finally ready to leave the road's-end rest house and move out in single file. Three Igorots were in the lead, single file. Then came Steve and Nina followed by three more Igorots who were followed by the six load-carrying Igorots.

At first there was a trail and the little expedition moved ahead at a fair pace in the early morning mist and fog. A slight breeze stirred the fog and gave the group an unreal appearance as they moved along. Birds chirped and now and then a monkey chattered at the invaders of their domain. Their route took them along the eastern slope of a high ridge of the Cordillera Central.

Steve and Nina stood out from the brown-skinned Igorots not only for their fair skins but because of the way they were dressed. Both wore shirts and shorts once white but now with a dingy appearance. Both carried fanny packs and bolos and Steve, in addition, carried a .38 revolver, the only handgun in the outfit. Clemente Lawig, one of the Igorots with no load, carried a shotgun that had seen better days. It was well kept amd glistened with lubricant, but showed the wear of many years of use.

No provisions could be made for getting a blood sample out. Steve was concerned that a sample might spoil.

"How will we be able to preserve the qualities we want if the blood sample cannot be kept whole and fresh?"

Nina explained, "Recently, a special battery-operated container has been developed. It has super insulation and will maintain 40° F for two weeks before requiring battery replacement. Alan gave me one to take along and I stuck it in my luggage along with some extra batteries. I would have told you about it sooner, but I completely forgot about it. Besides, we have been kind of busy-both day and night. Mind you, I ain't complaining, but the nights were more fun."

Nina handed Steve the container which was about the size of a one-quart thermos bottle, but that could contain a pint of liquid.

"Wow! We should have had a few of these along when we were in Africa. They would have saved a lot of trouble and expense."

Nina agreed, but said, "That sure would have been nice, but the darn thing hadn't been invented yet."

The column moved slowly through the jungle. The rain was almost constant, punctuated by brief steamy periods of sunlight that soon gave way to more drenching rain. The lead man hacked constantly with his bolo to clear a way for the small group. It was tiring work and the lead man changed frequently.

Mosquitoes buzzed and bit. Leeches crept into their clothing and had to be removed carefully to avoid sores that were difficult to heal. If the column moved 15 Km. it was a good day. Steve kept his Brunton compass in his hand most of the time to keep the group moving north. Without the compass, there was nothing to guide on, no paths, no blazes - nothing. Each night they halted and the Igorots constructed a vine- tied shelter from the abundant Anahau palms.

The Anahau palms stood about 30 ft. high and its 6 to 8 inch bole was uniform for almost its entire height. The bark was tough but the inside of the palm was soft and they could be cut down readily with a bolo. The frond-like leaves were

110   Wimpfen

pleated and pie-slice shaped. Each leaf was about 3 ft. long. The leaves were removed and stacked while the trunk was cut lengthwise into segments of it's circumference about 2 inches wide and perhaps 3/8 of an inch thick at their centers.

A shelter for a night was constructed rapidly. Four trees that made up a rough rectangle about 5 ft by 7 ft. were selected and the space between them cleared. Trees about 3-4 inches in diameter were selected and lashed with rattan to the corner trees about 2 ft. above the ground. Slats of the Anahau palm were afixed to the horizontal supports using behoko or rattan. Slats were spaced about 1 inch apart.

Then, working from this floor, more poles were fastened horizontally to the corner uprights to support a sloping roof. Palm slats laid horizontally on the sloping rafters were tied on about a foot apart. The pleated leaves were tied on. For Steve and Nina, this crude shelter had palm leaf walls on three sides to afford some privacy. But there was no way Steve and Nina could satisfy their longing for one another under the watchful eyes of the twelve curious Igorots. They were each alone with their thoughts as they lay on their backs under the protective overhang of their mosquito bars. The Igorots got along without any obvious protection from the buzzing skeeters that surrounded them.

The fire smoldered. Each evening a few of the Igorots squatted around the fire, alone with their thoughts. One, Clemente Lawig, with seven reclining vees tattooed on his jaw, glanced now and then at the shelter Steve and Nina occupied. Lawig thought, "Their heads would make a fine addition to hang from roof edge of my home. It would be easy to take them and I could be off into the jungle before anyone would know what happened." Fortunately Lawig's thought passed. The men drifted away from the fire to their shelter.

Nina lay awake in the cool of the dank evening. She thought, "What in the world am I doing in this remote jungle with a bunch of head hunters. My life is at risk and so is that of Steve and the child I'm carrying. This is sheer stupidity and for what?"

The next morning they were awakened as the Igorots chatted. Looking out they saw that the cooking fire had been stirred up and the iron pot was boiling as one man prepared to make rice. He counted them out and dropped handfulls of rice into the steaming pot. Soon the rice boiled and swelled and it was time for breakfast. Each of the twelve Igorots and Steve and Nina were handed an open can of fish to have with their portion of rice laid out on a palm leaf. They were all hungry and ate with relish.

As the pot emptied, the self designated cook, pried out pieces of the nearly-burned rice that lined the huge pot. Each person was handed a chunk of this caked rice. Then the empty pot was washed in the little stream that ran by their camp. The remaing gear, blankets and other things were soon packed and they were on their way.

Within a few weeks the jungle would reclaim the several palm shacks and the evidence of their passing would vanish. The next several days were replicas of that first day.

"I don't think I'll ever be able to eat rice and fish again." exclaimed Nina. "Three days with little else to chew on almost makes me gag when it comes to mealtime!"

"I know what you mean. I am fed up with this menu. I think I'll try to shoot a wild chicken so we can have something different with our rice."

"Great idea, but how are you going to go about it when we can't see ten feet into the jungle?"

"Oh, I don't plan to do it myself, Nina. I'm going to talk it over with Moclo and see if he can manage to get us something else to eat."

"Not a problem, Sor,"said Moclo."We have wide choice. Wild chicken, monkey, pig or deer. Which you like? We get."

"Wild pig would go good, Moclo. How do you plan to find one?"

"Oh, we no find Sor. Wild pig he find bayatik and we have him."

"What is this bayatik? I really don't understand."

"Bayatik is device we use for many generations. We take small bamboo and stick piece of fire-hardened bamboo on one end. Then along pig trail in jungle, we set two forked sticks to hold the bamboo spear in line with a small sapling. Bend back sapling and hold back with peg. The sapling, once released, will drive spear into target. Tie vine to peg and stretch vine across trail. Big surprise for pig when he come along trail. Many kind bayatik. Put spear higher if want to get deer or man. Anyhow, many of us get wounded by bayatik set for animals."

Moclo led Steve along some game trails in the jungle, Finally he selected a likely spot and quickly constructed a bayatik that would propel a three foot long spear into whatever tripped the device by moving the fine vine stretched across the game trail.

Every several hours Moclo or one of the other Igorots would check the bayatik and then one man came back carrying a bristly razorback that was soon prepared for cooking. The body cavity was filled with cooked rice and the pig was swung slowly over the hot coals by the two men that grasped the pig's fore feet and hind feet.

In several hours there was barbecued pig for dinner, a welcome relief from the canned pilchards. A selection of fresh papaya and mango added to the savor of the meal. Moclo offered another fruit the durian.

"This durian has fine taste. I know you like if you can get past strong smell." he urged. But the rank odor of the durian was just too much and they rejected even sampling the rare tropical fruit with a reported fine savor.

Each night in their anahau palm shack Nina and Steve rigged their mosquito bars and swallowed their quinine pills sluiced down with a shot of bourbon. They each slept under a separate net, but reached out to hold one anothers hand risking the attack of the hungry mosquitos.

Four days into the jungle they were awakened earlier than usual. They peered into the dimness of the before-dawn light and saw that their camp was surrounded by some twenty Pygmies, all at the ready with their bows and poison-tipped arrows. Now they relied on the one Igorot that could converse with the Pygmies. Soon the Pygmies lowered their bows and some faces were wreathed with tentative smiles.

The Igorot interpreter listened as the Pygmies chattered. Then he explained to Steve and Nina that the Pygmies came in peace and sought help for one of the Pygmy warriors who had been badly wounded by an unseen bayatik.

The wounded Pygmy emerged from the protective shelter of the jungle when Steve and Nina said they would do all they could to help the wounded tribesman. Primitive surgery was indicated to remove the spear embedded in the minute warrior's thigh.

Removal of the spear itself was no problem. Steve pulled it out and threw it aside. A Pygmy picked it up and spoke rapidly to the interpreter This Igorot turned to Steve and explained that the fire-hardened spear point was still in the man's thigh.

This was going to require more that Steve had anticipated. He gave the wounded man three Tylenol and by signs showed several of the Igorots how the wounded man should be held.

Steve took a single-edged razor blade from his pack and, using his lighter, heated the edge to a dull red. When it cooled he was ready. He stuffed rolls of bandage in the man's mouth. Holding the razor he cut deeply into the man's thigh to expose and extract a three inch long piece of bamboo.

Nina collected the blood sample they had come for. Although the wound and subsequent incision were painfully deep the Pygmy never emitted a sound of protest. Finally the job was done and after sprinkling the wound amply with antibiotics, the wound was closed using dental floss and a large sewing needle.

A litter was quickly constructed by the Pygmies to carry their wounded man. Bamboo poles and strips of behoko vine were tied together to make the litter that four men could carry. Steve and Nina were invited to join the Pygmies at their camp. The Igorots as well followed the Pygmies.

Coming to a rushing stream Nina had reservations about wading across. While she and Steve were debating the matter a diminutive Pygmy boy came along leading a huge Carabao. By sign language the boy indicated that Nina should climb on the Carabao and he would take her across the three-foot deep tumbling torrent. At first Nina tried to straddle the broad-backed animal but finally succeeded in getting aboard by sitting sidewise. With a few times of nearly sliding off the back of the Carabao, they finally made it to the far side. Both Nina and Steve heaved sighs of relief.

The Pygmy village consisted of a number of Nipa shacks and perhaps twenty five or thirty people, the families of the warriors that had startled the visitors. Tiny tots completely nude seemed to be in the majority. No one was hampered with clothing. The Pygmies lived a primitive life subsisting mainly on the small game the men would bring in and the abundant supply of papaya, mango, durian and other fruits of the forest. Nina was a cause for wonder. Although the Pygmies had seen white men a few times, this was the first white woman that had penetrated into the Pygmy lands.

The Pygmies didn't stay very long in one place. When the rewards of hunting an area began to decline, they would move camp to a new location five or six miles away and set up a new camp. They stayed in the extensive forest but ownership of lands was a concept beyond them. Steve wondered what would happen to the Pygmies as civilization would eventually encroach on the lands the Pygmies used.

When it was time to go the Pygmies were all smiles of gratitude for what Steve and Nina had done to save their wounded man. Steve got rid of most of the remaining articles that had been purchased for gifts. Then it was time to retrace their steps to the Land Rover.

Two days on the return trip covered far more ground than on the way out. There was a minimum of trail cutting as the jungle had insufficient time to reclaim the scars of the trail cut earlier.

On the third morning of the return trip daylight just didn't come. It wasn't possible to see the sky.

"It sure is a funny morning." mused Nina. "I wonder why it is staying so dark? "

Moclo and three other Igorots appeared out of the morning mist.

"Sor, big wind you call Typhoon come soon. We get ready. Must cover all gear and fasten down rain proof covers. We make shack strong and hope no blow away. These Typhoon bad feller. Do much damage."

The men worked fast to secure the anahua palm shack built for a one night stand. More behoko vines were cut and used to lash the flimsy structure to nearby trees and to tie down the rustling palm leaves of the sides and roof of the shelter.

The rain came pelting down and the wind roared through the trees. Loud tearing sounds were made by trees that were being bent beyond their breaking point. Conversation was impossible above the wavering high pitch of the wind, rain and crashing trees.

116

This kept on for an hour or more as Steve and Nina held on to each other in their shaking shelter. They were alone and wondered how their crew was making out as the vigorous storm increased in intensity. Their great concern was that one of the huge tropical trees might fall on and crush their shelter and them along with it. Then came a quiet time as the eye of the storm passed over.

Moclo appeared and explained what was happening and checked to see that his charges were getting through the storm safely.

"You stay close by shack. This not over. Soon wind return and blow from other direction. More rain, more wind, more trees fall." Moclo's predictions were accurate as the expedition was again under the lash of the deafening wind, pelting rain and the anguished roar of trees being uprooted and broken off as the pressures exceeded their strength.

Finally it ended and Steve looked out at messy tangled jungle. With all the deadfalls and the thick mud it was going to be harder to get back to Banaue than it was on their trip north. Fortunately they were unhurt and none of the Igorots were harmed. Their gear and the precious sample were all intact.

The return trip was tough going and very slow. They were almost constantly climbing over fallen trees that were too big to cut away. Their outbound trail had been wiped out. Other than being extremly arduous, the rest of the return trip was uneventful for which the sample seekers were thankful.

The group arrived back at the Banaue rest house exhausted late in the afternoon. Steve paid off the Igorots and gravely said goodbye to each one with a strong handshake. Each Igorot had been paid with a generous bonus. It was evident that the Igorots said goodby to their white friends with regret. After the shared experiences of the Pygmy trail, they had become attached to Steve and Nina.

The Landrover was ready and waiting.

"Look, Steve, this is a rest house. It has bunks and offers meals even if they are rather primitive. Never in my life have I had more need of rest. Let's just stay here a few days and try to recoup our energy. Right now I just can't face the trip back to Manila."

"You are absolutely right! Come to think of it I'm sort of exhausted myself. I think a few days or even more will do us more good than anything else."

That night they dined on rations that had been stored in the Land Rover.

"Gosh, I never thought corned willy beef could taste so good. And these canned potatoes are just out of this world. I don't ever want to see those canned pilchards and rice again!"

"I'm inclined to agree, Nina. But I think this canned spinach is the best tasting stuff I've ever eaten. Isn't it strange what a prolonged diet of fish and rice can do to one's taste buds?"

That evening they sat on the veranda and watched the passing scene. A strange twanging sound came from the trail down to the irrigated fields below the village. Soon a group of Igorot women passed each carrying a full basket of camotes. The sturdy ladies wore nothing on their feet and a tapis around their hips was their sole article of clothing. Their bare and well-formed breasts trickled with sweat and bobbed in unison as they trudged up the trail from the fields. The baskets were secured by a band of woven rattan that passed across their foreheads. The rattan passed around the narrower part of the cone-shaped baskets that rode on the bearer's back.

Each carried a devil stick that they banged on the palm of the empty hand. The devil stick was an 18 inch length of bamboo that was divided at one end so that two tongues of bamboo were left. These vibrated and hummed as the women used them to ward off devils and other evil spirits.

As they came out of the jungle and turned on the road towards the village, the four women shed their baskets and rested on a log.

"One of those devil sticks is just what I need! Maybe I could use it to ward you off, Steve, when you get too pestersome." With that she went to talk to the women who understood not a word. When Nina started to wave a few bills around and touched the devil stick of one of the ladies, the message came across. Reluctantly the woman gave up her precious devil stick in exchange for the bills Nina offered.

Returning to the veranda of the rest house, Nina amused both herself and Steve as she coaxed various strains from her own personal devil stick.

"After these several weeks, I am so glad that I was born in the good old USA. With the hardships of life here, it is no wonder that life expectancy is so low. Maybe all the children they bear has a lot to do with it. Still the population of the Islands keeps on growing."

They watched as a tall dignified Igorot approached the rest house. His expressive face was wreathed in a wide smile. A few gaps, where teeth were missing, showed in his grin. As he talked his bushy eyebrows looked like two caterpillars dancing. An iron gray mass of tousled hair crowned his head. The wrinkled forehead and eyes gave the man an air of wisdom. Heavy gold wire earrings were his sole decoration. The background of ancient rice terraces, provider for the tribe, was most appropriate.

"I Pip-Pitong chief of these Kalinga here. Tomorrow we have canyao. You come as honored guests."

"This could be interesting," replied Steve. "We accept your invitation with great pleasure."

"Canyao not here. Canyao take place in ceremonial place across water. Canyao not only honor you, our guests, but newly-wed couple."

They were both anxious to get back to Denver with their precious sample and to their privacy. But they knew that they had to accept Pip-Pitong's invitation to avoid offense. On the following day they headed out towards the ceremonial place when they came to a swift stream several feet deep with no easy crossing place. They walked up stream and then down stream without finding a safe place to ford.

A few hours after their arrival at the stream along came a lad leading a carabao by its nose ring. When the boy offered his carabo as transport, Steve and Nina readily agreed. They clambered aboard the buffalo's broad back and crossed the stream without getting wet above their ankles.

Soon they could hear the ring of the gangsas and the beat of the drums and followed the sound to the site of the celebration. The entire village was present along with groups from other nearby communities. The differences in dress, the patterns of the men's gee strings and the womens tapices were identifiable with the several tribal villages.

Steve and Nina arrived just in time to see the men perform a head hunting dance where a coconut carved to look like a man's head was mounted on a short staff. The twelve men involved carried either spears or head hunting axes. These had a point on one end of the wide blade and an inward curve on the other, truly a wicked looking instrument for perforation of the skull and the separation of the head from the body.

Men kneeling in the circle that surrounded the dancers beat methodically on the gangsas the round brass gongs handed down from generation to generation Most were about 15 inches in diameter and about two inches deep. Suspended from a leather thong they twisted as they were beaten with a short stick or bone. The drums were hollowed logs with a taut skin covering but some were made of hollowed logs on which a tongue of wood was left projecting over the void.

Young men with nose flutes provoked plaintive melodies that blended with the raucous beat of drum and gangsa. It was a fierce scene as the firelight glistened on the near-naked bodies of the agile dancers.

Women gathered to do a rice winnowing dance. The noise of drum and gansa almost drowned out the plaintive notes of the nose flutes. Young boys and girls did a suggestive dance reminiscent of the dances done at the oologs, houses of trial marriage.

Then the field was cleared and the carabao was made to run the gantlet between two rows of men armed with fighting bolos. Chunks of the poor critter were sliced off as the buffalo ran by and the dripping meat was passed to women standing behind the men.

What remained of the carabao was butchered and everyone had a piece of meat to skewer and cook on the several fires that had been built. Soon pieces of the slightly cooked carabo were tendered to Steve and Nina.

"Steve," whispered Nina, "I just can't handle this. That poor creature that took us across the stream. I think I'm going to be sick."

It was nauseating to both, but rather than create a scene, they each took a piece and, at an appropriate time, tossed the meat into the brush.

All the proceeding were conducted with ceremonious gravity to honor the newly wed couple. Not knowing a word of the Kalinga dialect, the guests were often puzzled by what happened. Then Pip-Pitong approached the pair holding a carabao horn that had been carved and cut to be a ceremonial cup.

"Here, friends of the Kalinga, is the Bilibud, our sacred drink." He extended the cup to Nina. With one whiff of the cups potent contents, Nina knew she could not stomach Pip-Pitong's offer.

"This is too great an honor for a mere woman," she said. "No female is worthy of drinking the Bilibud." With that Nina passed the horn to Steve. He was trapped. The vile smell of the nauseous liquid assailed his senses. But what to do. There was no escape. Steve held the stinking horn to his mouth but did not drink. He held his breath until he could return the horn to Pip-Pitong.

The Chief of all the Kalingas nodded gravely saying. " Now you are one us, a true Kalinga warrior."

When the opportunity came the pair escaped. On their return they splashed into the rushing stream and got soaking wet. In a short time they were back at the rest house, showered and went to bed, glad that the festivities of the evening were over, if not for the bride and groom, at least for them.

Early the next morning they loaded the Landrover and headed south. The Mountain Trail was a shambles. Loosened by the torrents shed by the typhoon, there were many mudslides that blocked progress. Crews of men and women were busy as ants in moving the slippery mass by dumping it off the roadside. It seemed like an unending task and as often as not, another slide would occur behind their Land Rover as they made slow progress over the worst part of the trail.

Another night in the Bontoc hotel and then they slid and skidded over the Mountain Trail to finally arrive in Baguio, tired and dirty. They looked forward to a meal with real food. Several days at the Pines Hotel found them sufficiently rested to proceed to Manila and then on to Denver.

It was with a sigh of relief that they turned the sample bottle over to Alan Muster so that his crew could make the essential checks to tag the genes that made the Pygmies what they were and to compare them with the genes from the two

122   Wimpfen

African samples. Months passed before that objective was attained

After a careful review of the mountain of accumulated data, Alan stated, "Now we know that the DNA, genes and chromosomes of the little people from the three areas are essentially the same. Genetic history has been made. We know much more than we had ever hoped for about the impact of various genes on their hosts."

Nina kept on with her work at the lab which now included the objective of making quantities of the serum that might be used to change the world. One major problem remained. How could they utilize the serum for the mass impact needed?

Nina continued to be active despite the minor swelling of her seven month's pregnancy. Finally the time arrived. It was an unusually easy delivery as the perfectly formed but tiny baby weighed a mere three pounds. Steve and Nina were elated! Their love had resulted in this newborn creature and, almost equal in importance, the little boy was proof that their goal of smaller people was attainable.

CHAPTER 5
WORLD OF CHANGE

"Let's call our son Noval? He certainly is new! I hope he can have a happy life even though he is unique among all the world."

"Hey, that's a great idea. But what a lot we have to think about so that our Noval doesn't become a complete misfit in a world peopled by folks nearly twice his size."

Noval was the first of what Steve and Alan and their mates hoped would be a generation of smaller people that would, in turn, repeat the progression towards the end that the entire world would become peopled with little folk. If they failed in this effort it would not be many generations in the future before the world population would destroy it's habitat and itself.

"It's awesome to think that mankind could pass into oblivion." said Nina.

"And that is most assuredly what's gonna' happen if we can't come up with a way, a successful way, of getting this 'smaller' serum into a major part of the world's population. Just like a bunch of rats confined in a box, we'll eliminate each other and turn the world over to the cockroaches. The dinosaurs were around for 150 million years, give or take ten million. They didn't destroy themselves. It took the impact of an asteroid from outerspace to do that. The demise of the dinosaurs was less cruel than what will happen if the world is overpopulated with what we laughingly call humankind." Steve was bitter.

"A few days ago while cleaning out some old files I came across a clipping from the Parade Magazine of 1996. It was interesting to reread that clipping." mused Nina. "Some guy asked Marilyn Vos Savant,'How many humans can inhabit the Earth and still maintain a decent standard of living,

124   Wimpfen

without having an adverse effect on the environment ?' She answered , 'This depends on what we consider to be a decent standard of living. In my own opinion, mere subsistence is not nearly good enough, and the upper-population threshold has already been reached. Even now, the Earth is badly damaged, but to bring the average diet of Third World countries in line with that of the United States, their food supply would need to increase by more than 400%. Without a major technological breakthrough, this is not possible. It is also not a minor, isolated problem. More than 75% of the world's population lives in developing countries.'

'Over the next 100 years, deforestation will continue, more topsoil will be depleted, and water supplies will grow increasingly polluted as the population doubles. (By then, an even *greater* percentage will be living in Third World countries.) At this point, the world population is expected to stabilize. However this does not mean planetary *resources* will be stable. They will not.'

'I believe technology will come to the rescue even if it means that someday much food will closely resemble feed instead. And will there be a decent standard of living then? I think so. But it would be much better if our population were to stop growing *now.*'

The big question was - How could they accomplish the major task of innoculation of the entire world population? Although the injection worked, at least in diminishing the size of babies of treated parents, how could this be achieved on a world wide scale? Injections could be offered in clinics throughout the world. But what prospective parents would go to a clinic to get shots that would result in their offspring being a 'shrimp?'

"Are injections the only way to go? Maybe there could be a pill that would do the job. Birth control pills were of some help, however small, in relation to world birthrates. Don't you think we should give that route a try?"

"You're right, Steve. With the overwhelming importance of achieving the goal, we just can't afford to leave any stone unturned. Your specimen mine is generating enough money so that we needn't poor-boy the effort. Let's get to work to see if we can develop an oral additive that will have the same effect as an injection. It was done years ago with cortisone, so we do have a precedent that was successful."Alan postulated.

Up to this point the work of testing with mice was done by injection, usually at the base of the underside of the tail. "Now we must find a way to get the serum into solid form and find a way to get the mice to injest the 'smaller' pills. Guess the first try will be by centrifuging the serum and drying the concentrated serum." mused Alan. Work on this idea began the next day with four researchers trying variations of the centrifuging method. Within a week a dry powder had been developed that would be tested on multiple pairs of mice.

" Won't we have to test the powder by using different quantities?" asked Steve.

"Yes, and that is the quick and easy part. Then we must wait and see what develops after the mice mate. Hopefully in 90 days, possibly less, we'll have some litters and can get a good idea as to whether the 'smaller' powder can be ingested to result in smaller progeny. Maybe we should take a vacation and go fishing. It's Spring and the trout should be hungry after the winter we've just gone through. Besides, we always seem to come up with some pretty good ideas when we sit around a campfire."

"I'm with you, Alan and I know just where we should go to have a ball. It's a bit further than our usual trips but I think you'll cotton to the plan."

"Just where do you have in mind. I thought you really enjoyed the fun we've had on the western slope streams and the Grand Mesa?

126   Wimpfen

"That's right, Alan. We've both had a ball in those spots. But up out of Silverton there are a few high country lakes that seldom get fished. They're hard to get to and take a bit of climbing. But they are full of wild trout that always provide stiff battles. I've been up there once before, but am not sure that I could find them. I'll get a topographic map of the area and then we can be sure."

"Sounds good to me. Let's get your old jeep out, stock up with some grub and take off. I'm more than ready for a couple of weeks away from it all."

Nina and Maria understood the needs of the two men and interposed no objection when they learned that their fishing trip might last several weeks.

"I'm looking forward to having some time byself."said Nina.

"Me too."was Maria's reaction. "It will be a like a new experience being without our husbands for a while. They may not know it but, for one, I appreciate having a bit of time by myself."

"I remember the name of one of those lakes. It is called Highland Mary after the now abandoned gold mine that is in the lower reaches of the canyon. That is where we'll park the jeep and then hoof it up to the lake."

Now the ruins of the old mine were below them as they paused and rested on the way to the Highland Mary lake. There seemed to be bench after bench each one several hundred feet higher. As they came to the top of each bench, they thought the lake would be there. After climbing many such benches, both Steve and Alan were close to abandoning the search. Finally they topped out a bench far above timberline in a blinding squall of hail and snow. When it cleared, there was the Highland Mary, the wind rippling the surface of the ten-acre lake. It was clear that the lake was seldom fished as it was just too tough to get to. With the first cast both men hooked fighting rainbows that were about 15 inches long.

They hooked and released trout for more than an hour and then lay down and rested while squall after squall of hail mixed with snow chilled them to the bone. They kept several trout for their dinner and then trudged back to the mine. It was harder going down the steep trail than it was going up.

Broiled trout, beans and bourbon made a filling meal.

Relaxing around the campfire in the chill of the August evening, Steve reflected,"Who would have ever dreamed that those fireside chats we had so long ago would have broiught us so far forward from those days of a distant concept. I'm real pleased that we had the gumption to seize the idea and run with it."

"Me too. I never had a clue that something like this would enter my life. Now that it has I have an inward glow of real achievement and believe we are going to take a giant step that will alter the world."

Further research proved that the serum could be ingested with the same results as an injection. It did require that several pills be taken.This was proven with mice and subsequently with dogs using a solid form of the serum in tablet form. But what a tremendous distribution problem?

"There has to be some way that the serum can be distributed and people inoculated without anyone making a choice for or against."

"There is one way that might work." said Alan, "For ages the world has been plagued by malaria and it is delivered indiscriminately to all by the anopheles mosquito. The anopheles favors warm humid climates. Yet mosquitoes of various types are ubiquitous.They'll drive you nuts everywhere in the world with the possible exception of desert climates. In Alaska I recall seeing the caribou hunt out patches of snow to stand on to avoid the skeeters."

"That's going to be a toughie."was Steve's comment. " It seems that we would first have to get the serum into the skeeters and then get them to bite folks. After that it would be a wait and see thing to find out if the system works."

"Getting the mosquitoes infected won't be much of a task. We can put a bunch of mosquitoes in a closed cage with one of the treated rabbits. Then, when the poor rabbit has been bitten enough, the mosquitoes should carry the serum and transfer it by biting someone just as the anopheles transmits malaria. Then it will be time to jump to humans!"

"It may be difficult to find a willing guinea pig that will put up with such a test. Who in the world will stand still to get bitten by mosquitoes with some unknown characteristics? And if that guinea pig were told that the objective of the test was to see if his procreative abilities might result in smaller than normal offspring,he would even be less likely to participate. Then too, we don't know if both parents need to have the serum in their bloodstream or will just one parent suffice. And if the prospective mother were aware that she might just possibly give birth to a midget, I just don't think she would be willing."

That evening Steve and Nina joined Alan and Mary for cocktails at the Muster home in Evergreen. To accompany the drinks Mary had prepared some unusual bocaditos - tiny empanadas filled with meat. They were spicy and promoted a thirst that encouraged each of the group to have another cocktail.

Alan munched on peanuts, one by one. He was silent and reflective. This went on for about 15 minutes when Alan suddenly spoke up.

"I've got it! Mary and I are the solution to this dilemma. For years we have been toying with the idea of having a baby and now is the time. I'm anxious to get mosquito bit and try making a baby. How do you feel about it Mary?"

"A great idea, Alan! I'm all for it. Just the other day I bought a red negligee and it is just the thing to get the ball rolling. Both of them I mean."

The scene was set. Early the following week Mary joined Alan in the laboratory. They each picked up a magazine and entered the small but comfortably appointed room where the treated mosquitoes were to be released. They sat there for almost an hour. For a while they read and then watched TV.

They were bitten several times. In their anticipation, they could hardly wait to get home. That afternoon, after lunch, they lay down.

As was his habit, Alan fell asleep as soon as his head hit the pillow. Mary lay awake and after a while gently reached into Alan's pajamas and began to softly caress the family jewels. Alan continued to sleep, but his erection grew to enormous proportions. Suddenly he awoke, all at the ready, and turned to Mary and lovingly caressed her. Soon they were locked into a tight embrace as Mary thought, "This is it! With such fire and all the semen I feel, this has to result in a take."

But their efforts didn't stop with that single passionate interlude. Every day Alan and Mary pursued their objective and there was no way of telling when conception actually took place. They had more fun and sexual exercise than they had experienced since the first night of their honeymoon. A few weeks later Mary announced that she was pregnant.

There was no way to determine if their progeny would be smaller than normal nor if the greed factor was eliminated. The whole subject of the greed factor was one of considerable concern but there was also a complete lack of any means of control. Was greed an emotion or was it something engendered in a child's upbringing? No one seemed able to put a finger on this objectionable characteristic of the human makeup. But it existed and was, perhaps, the major reason for most of the world's strife. It caused family feuds and wars, mayhem and murder. It would be a tremendous boon to all mankind if greed became eliminated.

Months passed and the evidence of pregnancy grew with the swelling of Mary's tummy. She stood proudly erect with her back curved as she pondered the future of the child she would bring to birth. "Would it be a boy or a girl? Would it be a smaller version of her and Alan or would it be an average-sized babe?"

Steve and Nina were equally anxious. Their injection had been direct with each receiving a shot of the serum into the arm. As a means of changing the world, this method had no merit.

The real secret of success rested with the outcome of the mosquito-bitten Mary and Alan. Impatiently, all four waited. It was promising that Mary's abdomen failed to reach the proportions that would be expected with a normal sized fetus.

"Did the future of the world hang in the balance?" pondered Steve. "Was a single mosquito bite to be the means by which the whole order of things here on earth would be altered for the better? Would starvation be banished? Would wars cease?" It overwhelmed one's patience as they all waited for Mary to come to term.

When Mary's time came it was actually an anticlimax as the two families felt certain that the goal of 'smaller' was within their grasp. Finally Mary delivered a fully-formed baby girl that weighed a scant three pounds. It was an easy delivery and both parents were overjoyed with the charming addition to their family. They named her Maria.

Now the researchers knew that their years of effort and painstaking tagging of genes was at least partially successful. Smaller humans were in the world's future.

"But what if the population of the world continues to grow at the rate of doubling itself in 40 years?" Nina queried. "Is there enough time to ward off the specter of wars over food and water, of famine and immeasurable suffering? It will take time to tell if sperm count and birth rates will be lowered."

Alan commented, "I shudder to think of the chaos that could result should world population burgeon from six billion to twelve billion by the year 2060! I hope that, in addition to peopling the world with smaller folk, events will confirm that our DNA manipulators had been successful in reducing sperm count. It might take several generations to determine if that goal can be met."

CHAPTER 6
THE ONSLAUGHT

The tiny Muster baby girl, the result of something more than a mosquito bite, compelled the researchers to action..

"We've got to produce the 'smaller' serum in quantities. Mosquitoes have to be propagated and treated and released world wide. Then we must find out if the offspring of the originally infected mosquitoes would still be capable of reducing the size of the offspring of the people they bite. It seems almost a superhuman task to do all the things necessary to achieve the 'smaller' goal."

"If newly-hatched mosquitoes fail to inherit the ability to inflict the 'smaller'genes in victims, the task of mass injection of the peoples of the world could require an enormous investment to keep creating new generations of effective mosquitoes." said Alan. "We've got a hell of a lot more questions than we do answers."

"You sure hit the mark there! Should we wait till we know if successive generations of mosquitoes carry the 'smaller' serum or should we proceed with massive releases of the treated mosquitoes so that generations of smaller people become propagated at the earliest possible date?"

Steve and Alan were appalled at the enormity of the task ahead. After several weeks of mulling over the multitude of interrelated problems, they decided to take a chance and release the 'smaller' mosquitoes towards the goal of world wide impact at the earliest possible date.

Then there was the question of how to accomplish the skeeter distribution. Should they travel the world and release mosquitoes in population centers? What about low-flying planes that would distribute skeeters here and there? It was a knotty problem and there seemed to be no effective way to send the mosquitoes on their world-saving mission.

It was Nina that came up with a solution.

"There just isn't enough money nor enough time for us to travel around the world releasing mosquitoes here and there. But there is a way that might work that would be just as effective and cost practically nothing."

"How?" echoed the others.

"Can't you see it? Here we are living in one of the world's largest transportation centers. It is a gamble, but if we released mosquitoes near the Denver International Airport gates, they would find their way to every corner of the globe!"

"That should sure have an impact! More than 50,000,000 people pass through DIA annually. They come from every corner of the world and could really spread the 'smaller' mosquitoes."

Soon one or more of the 'smaller' conspirators could be found at the Denver International Airport at any time, day or night. Wandering aimlessly around the air port, they would release a few of the doctored mosquitoes here and there from a ventilated vial. This inconspicuous introduction of skeeters would, possibly, change the future. Those that were carried to the tropical regions of the world would reproduce more rapidly and that was where they were needed most!

It was in the warmer climates that the doubling of populations was proceeding at a faster rate than elsewhere in the world. There were exceptions, of course, as Bolivia was expected to double its population in 27 years as compared with an average of 33 years for the population of all of South America to double. Should the skeeters have difficulty in reproducing and spreading the serum in Europe, it really didn't matter as much as the average doubling rate for all of Europe was 385 years. But the population of Europe was too large for the area of the continent. For example, tiny Netherlands had 1,300 person per square mile, Germany 650, Italy 525 and France 272. It was essential to achieve size reduction among the inhabitants of Europe despite its slow doubling rate.

Alan's lab at Denver University was busy with the task of determining if successive generations of skeeters would inherit the 'smaller' serum's ability to pass on the genes that caused tinier humans. And it just wasn't enough that the new generations would be about Pygmy height, the goal was to have the next generation about three feet in height.

There had been the concern on Alan's part that his superiors in the genetic research field might not go along with the objective of smaller people. After many long discussions, the research authorities at Denver University concurred with Alan's goals. Alan and Mary and Steve and Nina were commended for the progress already made and were urged to pursue their goals with redoubled speed.

The vice-president of research for the university commented, "It's unfortunate that we couldn't support your work towards its successful conclusion. But now we can again help and we want to be part of your effort." Alan and Steve agreed immediately.

The program needed all the help it could get if the decline of the US standard of living could be altered to avoid falling to the level of China's within fifty years and with still further declines foreseeable. The work of Alan and his associates was recognized as a measure that could stave off the sad promise of great chaos in the world's future.

Fortunately, research confirmed that the successive generations of mosquitoes inherited the 'smaller' serum. It had been feared that serum would work like the malaria infection. In that case the anopheles mosquito had to bite a malaria-carrying person in order to be able to pass on the disease by biting another person.

Alan, Steve and Nina met with the forecasting group at the university. Researchers there had been developing models for years in attempts to predict both short term and long term trends. They had finally concluded that the short term future was within the realm of predictability for as long as the assumptions held. Further, they had come to the realization that the future was beyond quantification no matter how much computer power was used towards problem solution. Still, it was worth a try.

It was basically important to determine the rate at which new generations would be smaller and the spread of the trend towards smaller people. Computer models were developed based on the sparse data available on the proliferation of the smaller babies that were now appearing world wide. These models were imperfect at best and only the passage of time would reveal the actual situation.

CHAPTER 7
DECADES OF CHANGE

Since the birth of Noval and Maria a decade had passed. Smaller babies were an accepted fact. Parents had become accustomed to seeing their offspring grow slowly. The eight and nine year old children were the first and oldest of the new generation. Although significantly smaller than most of their playmates of the same age, they were their intellectual equals. As more and more of the smaller children appeared, it was the larger babies that became the minority.

"Families are getting smaller." commented Nina.

"I wonder if that could be due to a lower sperm count or is there some other reason? We do know that the smaller folk are due to the serum, but I can't see why they're having fewer children." queried Steve.

Life had some newly imposed difficulties. There were the old "normal" children with siblings that were significantly smaller. Furniture just didn't fit. Doors were too big for the new generation. Cars were too large and steps too high. Looking ahead, elders could see that there could be many changes in the way things would be built. When people all became of a comparable size, houses could be smaller. All appliances could be smaller too. The impact on limited resources would be substantial as fewer raw materials would be needed for any given purpose.

Twenty years after the birth of Noval and Maria the world was, indeed, a different one. Many of the tall ancestors of the present day human race had died or were close to their ends. The children of the first of the smaller people resembled their parents in stature.

Noval Pringle and Maria Muster, as the first of the smaller folk, were unique as far as the rest of their generation was concerned. They felt the attitude of the larger children and, more often than not, stayed by themselves as they grew from childhood to adolescence and became adults. Neighbors throughout their lives and best friends as well, it was not unexpected when Noval and Maria decided to wed.

Noval had different interests from his Dad and decided to follow the field of geology. Maria too, departed from her father's field and claimed anthropology as her principal field of interest. Noval got his professional education at the Colorado School of Mines while Maria attended the University of Colorado at Boulder to pursue her studies in the field of anthropology. Both finished their formal college training and deferred marriage until the day after graduating. It was 2035 AD.

What a wedding? All present were attired to fit the occasion but it appeared as if two children were playing at wedding. There were the two principals, Noval about 3 ft. 6 in. tall and his bride a scant 3 ft. All the others were giants by comparison. This was the first wedding of the new smaller breed and was fully recorded with both still pictures and several different VCR tapes. A historical moment if there ever was one!

The bride and groom were at the center of all the jubilant participants at the wedding party. After partaking lightly of the feast, cake and champagne, the new couple changed into traveling togs and took off for the mountains. There, in the retreat specially designed and built by two sets of doting parents the newlyweds would embark on their new life. They drove slowly up through Red Rocks in the specially-fitted car Noval had enjoyed for some years. It was built to accommodate his height and enable him to reach and manage all controls.

At Empire they left the main road and headed north up the winding dirt road that took them to the site of the long-ago worked out Minnesota Mines. It was also the site of the closely guarded activity of recovering the rare gold-quartz specimens. Noval pulled up alongside of the cabin that Steve had built so long ago got out of the car and went around to the passenger side. Smiling at his bride, Noval lifted her out of the car and carried her onto the porch of the cabin and across the threshold. The first order of business was to get a fire going as the evening chill at 10,000 ft. could already be felt .

Noval found kindling and wood all ready on the porch and soon had a brisk fire warming the cabin. Noval and Maria sat before the fire silently still awed by their new relationship, the wedding, the party and the ride to Empire and their cabin.

Noval deftly opened the magnum of champagne. The bottle was close to a third of his height. He poured two glasses and handed one to Maria. They sat before the fire seeing visions in the flames and covertly glanced at one another. Shed of her outer travel togs, Maria was a vision of loveliness. Her tawny hair draped over her shoulders and fell, now and then, to conceal one or the other of her gray-green eyes. Nothing could conceal the impudence of her slightly turned-up nose or her flashing smile that so gladdened Noval's heart.

Maria's shoulders were straight and her breasts were full and firm. Her narrow waist dropped to fulsome hips above her long legs. As the fire warmed them, Maria kicked off her shoes and wiggled her toes towards the flames. Noval sat entranced at the beauty of his bride and he was happy, no joyful, at the aspect. As he sat, reflecting on his good fortune to have such a lovely bride, Maria got up, stretched, and moved to sit on Noval's lap. They had snuggled before and had warm petting sessions on many occasions,but always with the constraints of propriety hanging over them.

Now there was nothing to inhibit their love for one another. Noval nuzzled Maria's breasts and raised his head to kiss her neckand her hair. His caresses were returned with interest as Maria loosened his tie and eased him out of his shirt and undershirt. The fire roared and crackled in approval as Noval unbuttoned her blouse, unhooked her bra and lovingly caressed her well-rounded hummocks of passion. Her nipples were erect and hard as Noval lightly licked them. There were no restraints now! They rose and swiftly shed their remaining garments. Noval swept her into his arms and lay her gently on the bridal bed.

Maria was subjected to tender caresses and kisses over her entire body as she wriggled with pleasure and fondled Noval to an erection of unexpected hardness and size. Finally they could wait no longer and left their virginity behind as he joyfully entered her warm and moist vagina. Maria arched her back doing all she could to make the entry deep as they moved rhythmically to an extended and repeated orgasm. Their union was complete. As the night wore on it became complete again and again until they both sank back on the bed exhausted. When they awoke the sun was high on its course and their fire had dwindled to a few burning embers. Their joy in one another was unabated.

The 'smaller' researchers had long pondered the question of whether the engineered DNA with the specialized chromosomes and genes, would be inherited by the offspring of the first generation of smaller people. Now they didn't have long to wait. The ardent lovemaking of Maria and Noval on their wedding night and the subsequent weeks soon found Maria pregnant. Just nine months later she was delivered of a fine 3 lb. boy, a true replica of his parents.They were delighted by their offspring as were the grandparents.

All the researchers were elated as now there was confirmation that their work over the years could come to fruition towards the end that, within a few generations, the world would be populated by people that would make a substantially lesser impact on the globe's limited resources.

CHAPTER 8
A BRAVE NEW WORLD

The years that passed brought many changes to the world. Most of the people were small with average heights of about 3 feet plus or minus four inches. No new roads were being built. Automobiles were about half the size of the twentieth-century vehicles and consumed far less fuel to operate. More than half of the vehicles on the roads were powered by a combination of gasoline and electricity. The electric power was utilized in the cities. For long drives cross country the gasoline part of the vehicle was used. It also recharged the batteries.

What new construction was undertaken was designed and sized specifically for the smaller people of the time. Furniture and furnishings were likewise sized to meet the demands of the smaller folk. Farms were productive but many had fallen into disuse reverting to woodlands as their products were beyond the consuming capacity of the population.

Global population was not stabilizing. What was needed was a reduced sperm count. Population doubling rates had to change so that it would take four or five hundred years for the world's average to double. But that would never be realized until succeeding generations were close to the level of perpetuation rather than increasing. Families had to be smaller with rarely two scions and never as many as three.

Teams of explorationists roamed the far corners of the world to obtain data and take pictures to satisfy the continuing curiosity of man concerning his habitat. Islands of little change were found in several parts of the world. The Eskimos of the far north had not gone untouched and had developed into smaller people. It had been supposed by some researchers that the Eskimo might be immune to the 'smaller' serum because of their isolation. But most tribes

142

took summer excursions south and were exposed to the rapacious mosquitoes that plagued northern wetlands every summer.

Only in the fastnesses of Tibet and much of China were areas free of mosquitoes and there the inhabitants remained taller. They were remote from the rest of the world but had some exposure to the smaller people in their trading activities These islands of no change had little impact on the overall world situation wherein almost all the inhabitants were smaller and consumed less.

Traditional conflicts over land and water subsided as the smaller people required less of both. Navies and merchant ships of smaller dimensions were constructed with the raw materials salvaged from scrapping the monsters of past generations. Trains, however, remained of similar size as it was generally agreed that the existing trackage with its 56.5 inch gauge was serviceable and usable by the smaller people.

After all, this exceedingly odd number for a track gauge had come down unchanged for ages. For one reason the original railroad builders had once been tram constuctors and they used the same jigs and fixtures as wagon builders. And wagon-wheel gauge was set by ruts in ancient roads as attempts to run a different gauge in the ancient ruts would break the wheels on long hauls. They found it was better to stick with the gauge of those rutted roads built by Imperial Rome for their legions. These roads have been used ever since as rather than risk excessive wheel breakage, it was better to stick to the gauge of the ruts made by Roman war chariots. That gauge was established to be wide enough to accommodate the back-ends of two war horses.

As railway cars in passenger service wore out they were replaced with new equipment that could accommodate many more passengers per vehicle.

Armament, small arms and large were scrapped when their useful life was over. New weapons were designed for convenient use by the smaller people. Weapon calibers remained the same so that existing stocks of ammunition could be utilized. Sword and sabers were reduced in size for the smaller people.

Significant change took place in pharmaceuticals. Pills, gel caps, injections, everything had to be produced in sizes that matched the characteristics of the world's diminutive population.

Maria and Noval returned frequently to their honeymoon cabin north of Empire with their son Jack, the pride of the Pringles.The cabin was particularly convenient. Noval, following somewhat in his dad's footsteps worked as a geologist at the Henderson Mine. Maria chose to be a full-time mother and stayed at the couple's home in Golden and attended to the rearing of Jack.

On long winter evenings Noval and Maria delved into their heritage. They were constantly awed by the actions of their parents that had brought about the world-wide revolution by creating the smaller people of which they were the first. They were imbued with a sense of responsibility to do all possible to avert the perils of over population. They knew that they couldn't do much alone and funds were needed to engage the services of the many people required to continue the work initiated by Steve and Nina Pringle and the Musters.

Frequently Noval and Nina dined with either his or her parents or all six together. The conversations inevitably got around to discussions of the progression of the revolutionary concepts initiated by their parents.

Addressing his parents and in-laws Noval said, "You certainly accomplished wonders when you carried out your ideas so well. But where does the world go from here? Will it become overpopulated with us wee folk? Or. is there something that can be done to effectively control population?"

"We've been giving a lot of thought to that. We're trying to develop some ideas that could lead to the next steps to be undertaken and how they would be accomplished? Should animals be included in the plan to create smaller human beings? If not, then house cats could be a dangerous threat to the smaller people and dogs as well. What about horses and cattle? There are lots of questions to be answered and they all require money."

The main source of funds was the gold-quartz specimens from the mine at Empire. Over $40,000,000 had been derived from the sale of the rare specimens but now it looked as if the supply of the vug material had come to an end.

The original void that had probably caused the death of the two miners was almost exhausted. The two mummies had been removed and installed in an artificial drift that simulated the place where they died. This was at the National Mining Hall of Fame and Museum in Leadville, Colorado. That museum also housed two of the most beautiful of the gold-quartz specimens where they might be enjoyed by the many visitors to the Museum.

One bright fall day, Noval called home from the mine. "Maria, it's such a beautiful day and we have a weekend ahead of us. Let's meet at the cabin and spend it there. Jack will enjoy it. The aspen are turning and it'll be great fun."

"What a wonderful idea! Jack and I'll go pick up some groceries and we'll meet you. How about a charcoal-broiled steak for dinner?"

"Suits me fine," replied Noval, "Just so long as you can stop by the liquor store too. Our stock needs a bit of refurbishing."

Dinner was preceded by cocktails. As the sun set behind the high peaks of the Front range, Noval broiled their steaks.

The last rays of sunlight painted the tall cliff that lay to the right of their view, not far away. The air grew crisp and reluctantly they retreated to the fire that sparkled in the cabin's living room. Little Jack was soon asleep and the couple recalled the idyllic days and nights of their honeymoon.

It was easy to resume those passionate times of a few years back. Noval was proud of Maria and how she had carefully tended to herself and retained her pre-motherhood slimness. Perhaps her lovely breasts were a bit more full but Noval felt that they gave him just that much more to fondle. He particularly delighted in tonguing her erect brown nipples in the foreplay that gave them such fun. Before long they fell asleep in each others arms.

CHAPTER 9
CHANGE IN CHINA?

Kut Hing sat near the window in his HongKong office building overlooking Victoria bay and the tall buildings of nearby Kowloon. If he looked carefully, he could make out the yellow-colored ancient structure of the Peninsula Hotel, now preserved as a historical monument. HongKong had belonged to China since 1997 and the changes that had occurred since the takeover were significant.

Kut Hing was a part of this change. Shortly after the colony passed from Britain to China he had been assigned by Beijing to head up a network of operatives that spied on the western world and reported to the capital.

Kut lived on the outskirts of Kowloon and commuted daily by car traveling via one or the other of the three sets of tunnels that passed under Victoria Bay. Kut preferred to take the Western Harbour Crossing, completed in 1997, the first dual three-lane road tunnel in southeast Asia. It provided quicker access to West Kowloon and the new highways to Chek Lap Kok airport on Lantau.

China was huge and so were her problems. With 1.4 billion people, 25 percent of the world's population, China was the third largest nation of the world in area. It's population density of 300 persons per square mile was at a perilous level, but still expected to increase. Despite aggressive campaigns to control growth, China's population was expected to double in 60 years.

The Communist government based in Beijing was keenly aware of the spread of smaller babies throughout the world. China had not gone unaffected. But the authorities had concluded that they did not want China to become a nation of smaller people and mounted a major effort to bar entry of the serum that led in the direction of smaller people. All planes were fumigated before the passengers could disembark. Random luggage searches were conducted on all people entering China whether returning citizens or foreigners. The proliferation of the smaller babies was effectively under control and it was Kut Hing and his cohorts whose job it was to see that the agents of change were precluded entry.

China was made up of many tribes. To be sure that the country was fully covered in its drive to preclude the smaller people, Hing had recruited his staff and their minions from many of the tribes. There were Yak, Mi, Li and Miao from the south and southwest; Tibetan, Uygur and Kirghiz from the west; Kazak, Hui, Mongol, Manchu and Daur from the north; as well as the Ewenki, Korean, Tujia and Kaoshan from the east. Each one of the tribal members had two-way ties to the area of his origin. In this way the borders were covered to prohibit further entry of the 'smaller' serum. Although almost every tribe had its own language or dialect, they communicated with one another in the Han dialect known by more than 90 percent of China's millions.

Ed Chin, a trusted lieutenant to Kut Hing, was on top of what was going on throughout the country while Kut plotted and planned to assure that the people of China might be undiluted with any more of the smaller people.

"We have covered almost every possibility to keep our borders safe. With operatives at every port of entry, the program to seek out the smaller serum goes well."

"I, too, feel that we have every logical port of entry covered." replied Kut. "But what I fear is that entry may be sought in one or more of the thousands of possible illegal entry points along the coast or borders with adjoining nations. And I can't. for the life of me, figure out a way to make sure that such entry doesn't happen!"

"We have no way of knowing whether attempts might be made to bring the serum in through such entries. And we'll never know unless we could have a mole in the Pringle organization." commented Kut.

"That's a pretty big order. If we could place a mole in the Pringle camp, he would have to be an American, in appearance, in language and in custom. Such a person will be hard to find. What's more, he, or she, would have to be sympathetic to our opposition to the 'smaller' concept and be enthusiastic enough to take action to keep the Chinese from joining the ranks of the smaller people worldwide." reflected Chin.

"If it's OK with you, I'd like to discuss this with Dad. Our family had some emigrants to the US during his generation. We've lost contact with them, but Dad may have an idea or two."

"Go right ahead. It can't do any harm to talk to your father about distant kinfolk. He doesn't have to know what we are thinking about. You can make the conversation appear based on an interest in the family. Give it a try, Ed, and let me know how you make out."

Ed Chin, the number two man in Kut Hing's organization, was a country boy raised in the rice fields of Zhongshan, northwest of Guangshou. His tribe of Yao were somber hard-working farmers. Strong people, honest and dependable, they seldom ventured far from their home and fields. But Li Chin, Ed's father, had a brother, Tan, who was restless and who rebelled against the restrictions imposed by the Red Guard. Tan emigrated to the United States in the late 1980's and eventually became a US citizen.

Ed queried his Dad about this uncle and Li told him, "Yes, I think your Uncle Tan still lives. It is a place called California where he met and married another emigrant. They raised a family and prospered in the growing of strawberries and other fruits under the hot southern California sun. Tan doesn't write often, but in his last letter of several years ago, he mentioned his two sons. One of these boys, Tom, had become something of a problem. He had become an intense student of all things Chinese and longed to travel to the land of his ancestors."

"I should like to visit Uncle Tan and his family. How can I get in touch with him?".

"No problem, son, I think I know where I put his letter and it should have a return address." Li rummaged around in his desk and finally found the letter from his brother Tan still in its envelope. It carried a return address in Fresno, California

That was what Ed needed. As he drove back the 150 miles to Kowloon, he developed a plan that could, perhaps, bear fruit and provide the kind of information that Kut Hing needed in his efforts to preserve the Chinese from becoming another one of the growing number of smaller races. Perhaps, just perhaps, he could find a relation in California that was imbued with the spirit of his ancestors.

Such an individual would also have to be amenable to Ed Chin's idea that the Pringle organization could be invaded. A mole there would be of tremendous assistance in helping Kut Hing do his job of frustrating the miniaturization of the Chinese people. Looking ahead, Ed saw plenty of things that had to be done.

CHAPTER 10
FEWER?

Steve Pringle and Alan Muster were delighted with the way things were going. Specimens from the mine were going at great prices and they had no financial troubles in carrying on their work. The initial program was a huge success and there were only a few nations and areas of the world that had not been producing the smaller people engendered by The Pringle Progression

Now it was time to work on the other vital facet of the grand scheme.The sperm count of males throughout the world had to be reduced if the goal of an overall population reduction was to be achieved. A world over populated with small people was just about as depressing as what went on before. At the same time, it was essential that a greater effort be made to penetrate China with the carrier mosquitoes. There seemed to be a static situation in China. Smaller people were appearing here and there but the rate of change was much slower than in the rest of the world. It just wouldn't do to have an island of conventionally sized people especially in China with its one and one half billion population.The attack had to be made with greater effort to get the majority of the Chinese people inflicted with the 'smaller' serum.

Work at the research lab continued. The staff of some 30 people were researching various avenues of sperm count reduction. At the same time the treated mosquitoes were proliferating and being distributed at the Denver International Airport.

Every rumor, every clue as to a means of sperm count reduction was followed, most often with negative results.

Alan was buried in volumes of reports that were almost overwhelming. He commented, "Condoms, male and female, sponges,diaphragms, uterine devices, the pill have all been appraised. But the disturbing fact remains, if such devices aren't used, they damn sure won't impact the birth rate."

Steve concurred,"We have to discover something analogous to the 'smaller' serum that can be readily transported and inflicted on people without their knowledge. We have the precedent. Now it's up to research to come up with an applicable answer!"

The task was formidable. Further, it wasn't feasible to use humans for the tests. Mice were the answer. The animal wing had to be refurbished to house the new research work on the multitude of mice needed to determine propagation rates. This would require big bucks in a steady flow.

Fortunately, there was a still greater active market for the gold-quartz specimens. It seemed like every museum around the world wanted one of the beautiful and rare samples. Private collectors also were buying the qold-quartz specimens for their personal enjoyment. Specimens were still being mined from the original vug and development proceeded in the search for still another such 'jewelry store' vug. This development drifting was steadily increasing the reserves of high grade gold ore that could be mined at a future time.

Alan said, "There are many ideas of promise that we should examine. Of the many reagents we must test to control sperm count it appears that *Gossypol* offers some hope. *Gossypol* was developed long ago by the Chinese as a birth control pill. It was a derivative of raw cottonseed oil. The yellow pigment was made into pills. It had to be consumed daily until a total of about ten grams had been consumed by a male seeking birth control. But it seemed to go too far. Back in the 1970's *Gossypol* was linked to a host of infertility problems among rural Chinese that were taking the golden pills on a regular basis. It developed that

Gossypol, taken over an extended period, practically eliminated sperm without a reduction of testosterone levels. The pill poppers experienced no lesser libido or sexual ability. Wives complained that, while sex was still enjoyable, there were no pregnancies following. *Gossypol* practically disappeared from the scene as the Chinese authorities began to view it as anathema.

Gossypol seemed to be an alternative to vasectomy but was useless as a temporary contraceptive. Alan, his eyes weary from absorbing the details of many reports, said, "Raw cottonseed oil seems to be our preferred avenue of research. At least, it has a history of related success."

"We thought it was tough to develop the 'smaller' serum. It looks to me like this will be a still tougher job. There just isn't the time available to wait for generations to see if the scheme will work. There has to be some kind of a shortcut."

"In a way, there is. It may not be the best way, but we can use mice again to take a big step forward. They reproduce frequently and the gestation period is short. But we would still be working with tiny quantities. First, there would be the effort to extract various derivatives, as *Gossypol* was found. Then each potential extract has to be tested to see if sperm count is actually reduced. This requires running a standard that is untreated alongside of the mouse that has been treated with the derivative. When the mice copulate, samples of the ejaculate have to be recovered from the female and microscopic examination made to count the sperm"

"Wow, what a way to go!" blurted Steve. "That is going to take lots of mice, but I can see how we can shorten the time frame of study. But won't it be necessary to keep on examining the treated mouse with a lower sperm count just to see that there are no side effects?"

"Exactly. We have to find out if whatever we develop persists in keeping sperm count low. A temporary impact would be useless."

"There is another matter we'll have to act on soon. We're not getting any younger and we've been pushing hard for a long time. Maybe it's time to find somebody else to pick up part of the load. Someone who would have the same enthusiasm for the work."

"Our success with creating smaller people should prove that almost anything is possible. Their size has made a vast impact on the use of resources. But if we fail to get the sperm count down, the fateful days of the effect of population doubling will merely be delayed. Populations have to be reduced or the living standard of everyone will decline. Disaster could follow."

"Remember when the deer herd got so big up in the Arapaho Basin? The forage couldn't support that many deer and the first result was a scrawnier herd. Then along came a rough winter and most of the herd got wiped out. A similar situation could develop with respect to humans unless we get a handle on population control."

"We sure do have our work cut out for us. I've been thinking that we may not need to buy all the mice we'll need. As we're going to encourage the mice to mate so we can test their ejaculate for sperm, won't there be enough sperm left so the females can continue to bear litters? Another thing intrigues me. There are enough smaller people now that we could employ some in the lab. With their smaller hands, they could do a better job than you and I can in handling the mice."

There would be plenty of mice raised right in the lab once the program got going. But to start they needed to buy some of a strain where the mice were as similar as possible. In a Denver pet shop Alan found some inbred white mice that suited their needs and purchased a box of fifty females and another of fifty males for 75¢ a piece. They were to be delivered to the lab in Golden upon request.

Searching for more talent to conduct the search for a means of lowering male sperm count, Alan interviewed and hired a normal sized male, a Dr. Lee Chin and two 'smaller' people to serve as Laboratory aides. One was a pre-med student, a Dorothy Means, and the other a medical student majoring in pathology, Donald Janes. That increased the total employees at the lab to 32.

The morale of the team was excellent. During weekly sessions on Friday in the small meeting room of the lab, either Alan or Steve would talk about their goals and why they had been set. Questions would be answered and each subject would be discussed. In the end, these weekly meetings tended to weld the team together each striving towards the common goal of population control.

When the new wing was completed it contained the facilities for housing the mice, and separate compartments for copulation, called copcoms. Special labs were included where ejaculate would be extracted from the females for sperm count. The new researchers and their helpers had well-equipped space with computerized record keeping.

When the mice were delivered, they were each housed separately. As each test began, a male and female would be put together and closely observed. As soon as a male mounted a female, indicators set off a signal initiated by the extra heat generated. A researcher stood by ready to take out the female and extract some ejaculate which was immediately subjected to a sperm count. There were parallel sections of the lab so that mating pairs could be examined simultaneously. Facilities were available for the progeny as well.

But where to begin? Some *Gossypol* had been obtained from China. Work with mice treated with *gossypol* confirmed that sperm was virtually eliminated when a male mouse had consumed 12 milligrams of *Gossypol*.

"The fact that *Gossypol* was extracted from raw cotton - seed oil gives us a clue." mused Steve. "Maybe we should be examining other seed oils to see what develops?"

"Then there is another concept that could warrant further investigation." offered Alan. "Somewheres I know I read that some researchers at Duke University discovered that sperm cells have noses or at least the same molecules that the nose uses to detect certain odors. This work could lead to the develoment of new contraceptives. If spermatazoa sniff out eggs instead of just blundering into them, it might be possible to develop a drug that blocks their ability to pick up the egg scent. Perhaps some effort should be made to track down the 'perfume' emitted by the egg?"

So the main lab embarked on extended research into a variety of seed, including, sunflower, canola, sesame, achiote, dill, fennel and others. Pepper seeds were also studied and the wide varieties of chiles with their special properties was another avenue of research. A variety of extracts were derived from the many oils pressed from different seeds. These were compounded into tiny pellets that the male mice would consume with their food.

After each extract had been consumed in the amount of ten milligrams, the males were placed together with a female in a cage adjacent to a pair where the male was untreated. Semen was extracted from each female and the sperm counted. The similarity of the hybrid mice, it was hoped, would eliminate any bias on the tests. Record keeping on these experiments was a monumental burden. Several new computers were purchased to handle the additional work load. There were many failures as test after test showed no reduction in sperm count. In a number of cases the specific seed oil extracts were fatal. Some even increased sperm count!

Varying amounts of extracts were tried when there appeared to be a reduction in sperm count. The tests were pursued for many months. Finally there was a break-through when a certain sesame oil extract resulted in consistent reduction of male sperm on the order of 50%.

"What an achievement! I thought it would take much longer." exulted Steve

"If it hadn't been for that obscure fact about *Gossypol* we might have started on an entirely different route and gotten lost in the maze of data that would have piled up. I think we ought to call the new serum *sesaprik!*" "I like that," said Alan, " but don't you think we ought to try it out on Lee and his crew? After all, they did almost all the work that led to the discovery."

Lee Chin and his smaller helpers, Dorothy and Donald came in to Steve's office.

"We need to pick a name for the sesame seed oil derivative that reduces the sperm count in mice." said Steve, "I've suggested *sesaprik*. But as you three conducted the research that resulted in this serum, Alan and I think you should have a say in naming the stuff."

Dorothy objected to the prik suffix maybe because she didn't have one "With what she did have," thought Steve "she could get all the pricks she wanted."

"I think that sesaprik is just too suggestive. What would you think of sesamite as a name that might not prove offensive to anyone?" suggested Dorothy. Steve hated to abandon *sesaprik* but was outvoted and the new drug was dubbed *Sesamite*..

Repeatedly, they had proven that *Sesamite* was effective in reducing sperm count. A single oral dose did the job. But what worked on mice just wasn't enough.

Alan mused, "We have demonstrated conclusively that *sesamite* works fine on mice and that a single 15 milligram dose creates an effective 50% reduction in mouse sperm.

Now we need to have some human tests to see what happens. We need a vigorous male who is willing and a female who will cooperate. And this test cannot be just an "in and out" arrangement. We have to house these people, feed them and urge their mating under controlled circumstances. It doesn't matter to me if they aren't married to each other but I suppose we should have a married couple to assure there would be no third party interference."

"Even if the couple is married," mulled Lee, That's no guarantee that there might not be interference from a third party. We must have a woman who has sex exclusively with the male being tested, who will copulate frequently and submit to our sample taking immediately following each coupling."

Dorothy added, "How about the male? He has to be ready and willing and be ever ready for sex. Also, it would be a good idea if he had already fathered all the children he wanted. It could turn out that *Sesamite* was similar to *Gossypol* and render its consumer sterile."

Donald had been listening carefully to the discussion. "It could be that we could get the semen samples from a guy who would masturbate and get a sample from each time. That would place no woman at risk. Of course, we would need more than one man for such tests."

"All of these ideas have merit," said Alan, "and we should probably vary the procedure in several ways to be sure our work is without flaws."

It was easy to recruit men for the task. Several college students were intrigued with the idea and needed the pay to further their education. A comfortable room was fixed up in the main lab building and equipped with Playboy, Penthouse and several more lurid publications. Film strips and CD-ROM disks rounded out the collection of excitable material.

Private rooms adjoined the display room so the men could do their thing in privacy. This method eliminated the need to poke around in the vaginas of the partners of men being tested.

The scheme wasn't working too well. The two dimensional magazines and films just did not have the ability to keep the young men producing semen at the desired rate. Equipment for 3-D movies was obtained and these films seems slightly better. "There has to be a better way!" said Alan. "We need some full-sized three dimensional females to get the semen spurting."

"And just how do you propose to get some females that will put up with what we're trying to do here? Where will you find attractive dames that are going to expose themselves to sufficient appropriate action to get these young men to ejaculate?" asked Steve.

"I really don't think it will be that hard. The pay will be good and steady without them having to wait on a willing John. Also, the surroundings are better. What's more, these college students aren't exactly unattractive. Let's tell them what we are looking for and let them go out and recruit the girls."

"We have nothing to lose going that route. So let's get on with it!"

The three college students, Mike, Dick and Bob had been well indoctrinated in the objectives of the program, but felt that the two dimensional and audible stimulants just were not enough to keep them ejaculating at an adequate rate for the tests. They were delighted that they would have some three dimensional playmates to encourage their efforts.

"Isn't this a fun job!" Mike allowed. "Now we gotta' get out there and find us some playmates. Let's each of us recruit one and so we don't all come back with the same type, let's agree on goals. I'll go for a blond, Dick you find a redhead and Bob, you hunt up a brunette. But don't take that too literally Bob. The up-hunting will take place after we all get together and sampling can be carried on."

"Sounds good to me! But don't you think we should have a few more criteria? I suggest we look for the 21-15-21 types in the range of three foot two to three foot ten. And they ought to be lookers too." said Bob.

"OK let's go for it. We'll really have a time if we can find impassioned babes that'll give this chore their all!"

Mike was a tall 3 ft. 5 in. brunette with broad shoulders, a slim waist and a near constant grin. He was a student at Denver University where he played football and indulged in other athletic activities when he wasn't studying towards a degree in English. His long range plans called for getting a job at some western university, marrying and having a family. His conversation was well salted with quotes from major English authors going back to Chaucer. His personal attractiveness and outgoing manner promised that he would have no difficulty in finding a willing partner for the Pringle project.

Dick was also a Denver University student, an accounting major. A shock of black hair crowned a face that was both mobile and reflective. A serious student, he spent most of his time studying and working part time for an accounting firm. Dick stood 3 ft. 3 in. and was well formed. A shy smile made him attractive to the girls in his classes and he already had ideas as to whom he would approach as a partner.

Bob was a different type. He attended the Colorado School of Mines as a freshman. He had not yet gotten adjusted to college life and majored in partying and having fun. At 3 ft 7 in he was in demand by the basketball team and spent more time with his team and girls than he did with his books. His parent hoped that he would finally settle down and get his degree in geological engineering. Bob's outgoing personality assured his success in finding a willing partner for the project.

All three had their faces slapped a few times but their persistence paid off. Within a few days each of the young studs had recruited a girl from one of the many colleges in the area. Mike found a luscious blonde called Sue who was about 3 ft 4 in. tall with lissome curves and a will to really further the project. Dick's search resulted in recruiting a glorious red head with bright blue eyes and a playful spirit. Her name was Pat and she was enthusiastic about their goals. Tanya was the brunette sold on the project by Bob. He was looking forward eagerly to working with the well-rounded biology major.

Facilities within the laboratory were modified to provide living and working quarters for the six little researchers. Bedrooms for each were set up around a main sala equipped with a hot tub, a sauna and bathing facilities. The sala was furnished with radio, television, compact disk player and sufficient futons of varying sizes so that the sampling effort could take place spontaneously. An ample supply of colored condoms in red, blue and gold were available with a color assigned to each of the studs. That would simplify record keeping.

"Color-coded condoms just aren't enough." Alan pointed out. "Each specimen must be tracked and that means each one has to have a unique number We'll need to stamp an indelible number on each condom."

"We're going to have to keep track of time too. Let's give each of the working staff a date/time stamp and just before use, assuming he can remember to do it, he'll stamp the condom about to be used."

An adjoining room had computers, desks and all that was needed for analysis and keeping track of the sperm generated by the three males. It also had a one-way glass window for observation. Chin and his aides didn't want any shirking on the job!

The first day was uneventful; the girls were dressed discreetly and the three young men wore shorts. Much of the time was spent in examining their quarters and other facilities and chatting with their new-found friends. But not one forgot what they were there for and pairing off with their selection, they retired early. It was an active night replete with squeals, oh's, ah's and other odd noises. The next day the laundry department reported that linens from two of the workbenches indicated their use by virgins. Examination of the ten condoms used that first night confirmed the fact.

After a few day, it was noted that all of the condoms were not time and date stamped. Lack of this data could impede proper evaluation .

"We just can't tolerate not having this bit of information!" uttered Steve.

"I know, but what in the world can we do about it? In all the excitement of mating with a luscious willing partner maybe we're lucky that the boys remember to put on condoms. I was young once, and believe me, I know how they feel."

Pat was late in remembering that Dick had neglected to time/date stamp his condom after it was already installed on his erect apparatus.

"Put that thing on the table and I'll fix it!" said Pat

Not wanting to lose any time, she picked up the battery - powered stamp and placed it against the condom and pressed the activating button.

"Ouch, that hurt!" cried Dick. "Let's not forget to stamp that thing again. Stamping after installation is just too painful"

Despite the pain Dick's performance was OK and a useable sample obtained.

"There ought to a way out of this problem." thought Alan. "But we need some help. You know those condom dispensers that used to be found in filling station men's rooms? Perhaps if we got in touch with the manufacturer of those mechanical monsters, they might have an idea or so?"

The next day they spent time in going through the Yellow Pages and found several approaches. Telephone calls to the list finally came up with a company that had, at one time, made the condom dispensers. It was interested in the problem and shortly came up with a solution.

The new dispensers were installed in each of the young men's bedrooms. Without the need of a coin, one could just reach out and take a color-coded condom that was imprinted with it's unique number and stamped with the date and time.

"Now, we have to depend on our young studs not to get carried away. If they have some unnumbered matings. we'll never know about it. Let's hope they will remember." said Alan.

The study of *Sesamite* was under way and the semen samples from the first night served as part of the base-line study. There was less restraint the second day when Pat appeared in an enticing lava-lava; Sue wore only a waist high sarong and Tanya nicely filled a pair of shorts and a halter. Such clothing was easily shucked whenever the three pair were ready to create samples. Some 32 samples were collected in the first two days, enough to constitute an adequate base. The semen count in successive samples varied within acceptable limits and showed no reduction in sperm count despite the frequency of sample generation.

Now it was time to begin the *Sesamite* testing. Both oral and injectable *Sesamite* were under test. The initial dose was held to 5 milligrams and the results tabulated. It wasn't until the treatment level reached 15 milligrams that the first change was noted when Dick's sample showed a 10 percent reduction in sperm count. Medication was withheld for several days, but Dick's lower count stayed steady. Then it was time to try a slightly larger dose. Comparative studies between injections and oral doses disclosed no measurable difference.

Within a few days, it was noted that Dick was falling behind Mike and Bob in the number of samples provided.

"Let's get some competition into this effort." proposed Steve. "If we offer a graded bonus to each couple based on number of samples, that could serve to generate more. I think we should offer something like $10,000 for the most samples, $5,000 for runner up and $3,000 for third place."

"Hey, that's a great idea! And I won't argue with the numbers. But I think that one of the small quartz-gold samples as an added premium should promote more erections and injections."

Competition increased as each stud was encouraged by the bonus award, which went in equal amount to his companion. Their prowess was legendary. Each pair was doing its utmost as they strived towards an effective reagent that would reduce sperm count.

The end of summer was appoaching and the six students knew that their idyllic life as researchers would soon end. There were hundreds of samples that had been studied and more spawned each day. Modesty had vanished and often all three couples could be seen on the sala futons working away to produce samples. It had been discovered that a single 30 milligram dose of *Sesamite* would effectively reduce sperm count by plus-or-minus 50%. The three girls were pleased that their seductive efforts had such encouraging results Each of the three wanted to try tests without condoms, but their concern over the possibility of pregnancy proved to be an effective deterrent

By Christmas time, the lab learned that the three couples exciting summer had so endeared them to one another that each pair became man and wife. This was a great relief to Nina and Mary who had held many reservations about the unlicensed sexual orgies that had taken place during the summer.

Now there was work to be done to transfer *Sesamite* to the mosquitoes in such a way that a single mosquito bite would successfully endow those bitten with both the *smaller* serum and the *Sesamite*. The year was nearly over before success crowned the researcher's efforts.

CHAPTER 11
THE CHINA SCAMPER

Lee Chin was mindful of his commitment to Ed Chin. On a vacation trip to China, he met with Ed in Hong Kong and reported on the results of the Golden tests, *Sesamite* and the new breed of mosquito.

With one fourth of the world's population, China was determined to maintain the size of its people. With such a physical disparity, it would be easier for China to achieve and maintain world dominance.

"The Pringle group is bound to attempt to introduce the new mosquitoes into China!" affirmed Ed, "And we have to redouble our efforts to stop such an invasion."

"I would like to help and perhaps I could if I knew just when and where an effort might be made to penetrate China. But my work has been principally in research towards development of *Sesamite*. Distribution of the life-changing mosquitoes has been done strictly by the Pringles and Musters." said Lee.

"You might not know exactly when or where the invasion would take place, but you should have an idea if that gang is going to make an attempt on China. If you can determine that and let me know, we can take care of the problem from here." explained Ed.

"We must find a way to get the skeeters into China!" said Steve. "So far, they've been successful in stopping introduction by plane. Their practice of spraying each arriving flight has kept the skeeter penetration low, too low for us to meet our goals."

"There has to be some way we can get the skeeters in and I think I know how to do it. It isn't going to be like releasing mosquitoes near departing flights at Denver International. The target of China is so big along with the long term hazards of having one fourth of the world's population larger than the rest of the world, that we have to make an extra special effort to affect the Chinese."

"OK, Alan, I think we can agree on the importance of getting to the Chinese, but just what do you think is a way of getting the job done?"

"Well, this is what I have in mind. We'll prepare several special containers that will hold the skeeters and keep then alive and active for at least two weeks. These containers will be thin and curved to fit tightly above the hip. Each one will be tailor made for the person that will carry it."

"You and I will fly to Taiwan where we will either charter or buy a boat capable of navigating the coastal waters of China. Then we head for isolated coastal inlets along China's coast, go ashore, release the skeeters and get out quickly. It is going to be expensive, but I think it will do the job."

"That sounds good to me, Alan. But what if it doesn't work? In any event, do you think it wise to rely on just coastal releases? Maybe we should make some overland approaches? We could get to China via Viet Nam, Nepal, Pakistan, or Mongolia, for example. In that way the releases of the treated mosquitoes from a number of different places should increase our chances of success."

"You're probably right, Steve. Maybe three points of entry might be the way to go. But there is another thing that's bothering me. China has been so effective in stopping entry of the skeeters so far, I feel they would go to almost any lengths to assure their future as standard-sized people. Thus we should be thinking of keeping our plans secret so that there won't be any leaks that could result in thwarting our efforts."

"We could keep the plans entirely within the family."

"And that is the only sure way of making entry into China without leaks. It also means that you and I and Noval, as well, will have to be the ones that do the traveling and introduce the skeeters simultaneously."

Late one lazy Sunday afternoon Ed Chin telephoned Kut in Hong Kong.

"I know there's something going on and I suspect it's an effort to introduce the new brand of mosquitoes into China."

"What makes you think so?"asked Kut.

"Well, three of the family members are booked on Japan Airlines to fly to Tokyo next week. On top of that, in the lab we have been preparing some special containers for mosquitoes that are thin and curved and could be concealed on a body without much trouble."

"Do you have the date and flight number?" asked Kut.

"Yes, it's JAL 139 on Thursday June tenth." It was the year 2040.

"Thanks, Ed, that's good to know. We'll do what may be necessary and say, forget about this phone call."

When Steve and Alan and Noval and Maria arrived Tokyo they were not aware of the twelve operatives that Kut Hing had sent ahead to follow and observe the travelers. Kut's spies were unobtrusive but managed to learn that Noval and Maria were bound for Ulan Bator in Mongolia, while Alan headed for Kathmandu in Nepal. Steve was bound for Taipei in Taiwan.

Kut's operatives split up with four men following each of the traveling groups. They had their orders to follow and to destroy any suspicious containers that could be carrying mosquitoes. They were to carry out their mission without harm to the people involved unless that was unavoidable.

After a few days rest in Kathmandu, Alan began his preparations for the trip to Nyalam in China via a high pass in the Himalayas where the sole road entered China. He didn't expect any difficulty. He obtained a tourist visa and rented a car and driver for the short trip across the border.

It was only about 60 miles to Nyalam where Alan planned to release the contents of the two containers strapped to his waist. He was both surprised and shocked when he was subjected to a thorough search at the border and confiscation of the two containers. In addition, he was turned back to Kathmandu with his visa revoked.

Noval and Maria landed at Ulan Bator and stayed in their hotel several days. As with Alan, they were unaware of the four Chinese operatives that followed their every move. To get to the Chinese border one had to take an unpaved road for 450 miles southeast of Ulan Bator. It was going to be a rough trip. Noval was able to rent a Land Rover equipped with extra gas tanks. There was no trouble in obtaining tourist visas for himself and Maria.

They spent several days in finding a tent, sleeping bags and other gear. They purchased food and water containers as there was little to be found in the few small settlements along their route to China. Finally they were able to get on the road to complete their mission of releasing the mosquitoes at Erenhot in Nei Monggol, the north central state of China.

Two days out, in the Gobi Desert, en route to the border, the young couple found their road blocked by four pickups in a place where there was no opportunity to get around the barrier. Four armed men got out of the blocking vehicles. They were armed with assault rifles. Almost twice the size of Noval and Maria, the four bandits presented a fearful threat.

"Get out of your truck!" the bandit leader said. His tone was calm and his voice low yet commanding. His English was unaccented.

"You," he said, gesturing to Noval, "get over there." pointing to his three cohorts..

Noval did as ordered and was promptly subjected to a thorough search. Both of his special life-support mosquito carriers were found. One of the men threw them on the ground, while another poured gasoline on the two carriers and ignited them.

"Get back in your truck." they were told. "You may go wherever you wish." said the bandit leader as all four returned to their pickups and drove off in a cloud of dust towards the nearby Chinese border

Noval and Maria stood holding one another, still in shock from the sudden raid and the destruction of their mission. There was nothing left to do but to return to Golden in defeat.

CHAPTER 12
FINAL GOAL

Steve wandered about Taipei. His movements were slower as his advancing years took their toll. He thought back on all that had happened in his life and a smile of satisfaction came to his face. He wandered without apparent purpose enjoying the sights and smells of this vigorous port city. Steve made frequent stops as his curiosity was challenged by items in the storefront of one shop or another.

He took notice that he had a retinue of four men, similarly dressed in black suits, that contrasted with the bustling populace of Taipei. Each time he looked back it was apparent that these strangers to Taipei were bent on following him. At times, Steve noted, one or the other of these followers would pull out a notebook and scribble something in it. Whatever Steve was interested in seemed to be of concern to the following four.

He suspected that his hotel room might be subject to search. Each day, before he left his room, Steve would fasten a hair across the desk drawer and the other drawers in his room. One day he returned to find every hair broken. There was no other sign of the invasion of his hotel room. The Chinese were extremely careful!

It was without surprise that Steve opened letters from Alan and Noval who advised of the failure of their missions. Now it was up to him and Steve planned to move carefully and cautiously. The fate of the world rested on the success of his mission to release the treated mosquitoes on Chinas' shores.

Steve's interest turned to the docks where deep-sea vessels were unloading timber, copper, steel and other raw materials. Other vessels were loading finished products such as electronic items, white goods and a host of other things. These ships were destined to all parts of the world. On down from the big docks were marinas for smaller vessels and fishing boats. Steve decided it might be relaxing and fun to spend a day fishing.

One smiling fisherman captured Steve's attention. His wrinkled face was wreathed in smiles as he chattered some Chinese at Steve. Steve smiled back and raised his hands in supplication to indicate his not understanding. They were able to use sign language and head shakes to agree on a fishing trip for the following day.

Steve appeared at the dock early but his fisherman was ready and waiting. The old launch moved slowly out of the harbor as it's inboard Chevy engine chugged along. It was no surprise to Steve to raise his binoculars and see his four shadows put out not far behind. All day long, as they fished, the following launch was visible. How boring it must have been to sit on the horizon and watch an old Chinaman and an older American bait their hooks and now and then pull in a fish. Steve was enjoying himself and decided that he would impose further boredom on his trackers by a few more days of fishing.

Evenings Steve spent mainly in his room poring over maps of the China coast and caring for the caged mosquitoes that were always with him in their thin curved cages. It took a lot a map study but finally Steve found what he wanted. Down to the docks again he purchased a small speed boat that was adequate for the 150 mile trip across the Formosa Strait to the special spot he had selected as his target on the China coast.

Finally the day arrived for Steve's trip to the coast of mainland China. For days all had been ready and the launch equipped. He knew that as soon as he left Taiwan waters that he would be on his own in either escaping or fending off Kut's operatives. With every hope that it might prove unnecessary, Steve purchased a high caliber rifle equipped with a 6 power scope. A .38 caliber handgun completed his

172   Wimpfen

armament. He was ready to go. Extra fuel cans provided sufficient gasoline for the trip to China and a return to Taipei. His plan was outlined to Nina in a phone call.

In the early morning mist, Steve left Taipei harbor and headed west. Two hours out, he noted that a large launch appeared on the horizon, miles away. The seas were calm and it was most pleasant as Steve's launch moved steadily westward. By four in the afternoon Steve was approaching his targeted landing spot, a small village outside the town of Xianyou in Fujian province.

If his timing and the tide were right, Steve's launch would cross a shallow bar as he entered a narrow embayment. Moving at a cautious 20 knots, Steve scraped over the shallow reef that barred use of the narrow bay by fishing boats. He noted with interest that his pursuers were closing in and had been ever since he had come close to the China coast. Steve accelerated and so did his glue-like followers.

Their deeper-draft launch slammed into the reef, holed and began to sink. The frustrated Chinese began to fire at Steve as their launch settled in the water. Steve laughed to himself and headed up the long bay. He looked back to see the four armed Chinese floundering on the shallow reef as they struggled to reach the north shore of the bay. Steve kept on for four or five miles till he found a sandy beach that suited his needs.

Steve beached his launch on a sandy strip on the south side of the bay. It was an isolated spot. No house and no one were in sight. He carefully unbuttoned and removed his shirt and the band that held the two body-shaped mosquito cages. The tiny critters buzzed loudly, eager to escape the confinement of the shallow cages.

Gently Steve laid both cages on the sand and carefully opened each one releasing a small cloud of mosquitoes that took off in all directions to find nourishment. They didn't have far to travel to reach a nearby settlement. He wrapped the empty cages in the band that had held them next to his body. A few rocks were added to the bundle that Steve flung into the shallow bay.

Kut's operatives would soon be on his trail. He had a few miles head start. He stuffed the small backpack with his emergency rations, a change of clothing to blue baggy trousers and an ill fitting Mao jacket and the .38 revolver with extra ammunition. There was enough food stuff to last several days.

He left the launch as a reward for whomever found it and headed out. The whole night was before him to make good his escape..

"Where to go?" thought Steve. "I've got to have a plan! Perhaps I should head for Hong Kong, but that's 400 miles away. Somehow, I must keep moving to stay alive. I'll travel by night and hide by day."

As the sun set, Steve smiled to himself. "Now almost all the world is exposed to the magical impact of our buzzing skeeters. The Pringle Progression will continue."

"But I've got to get out of here, and quick! Those thugs following me are half my age or less. There's no way I can out run them. Maybe I can outwit them someway?"

Streve knew from his long hours of mapwork that about 90 miles to the west were the Daiyun Shan mountains rising almost 6000 feet in a series of rolling ridges. The range had long been worked for its scattered tin and tungsten deposits. In the pale moonlit night, Steve followed a narrow dirt road through the rice paddies that nearly covered the coastal plain. He wanted to get as much distance as possible between him and his pursuers.

Towards dawn he saw a flickering candle light in the window of some rice farmer. He approached the cottage with care. He was concerned that the coming encounter go well. He wanted to avoid startling the farmer. Softly he whistled a

174   Wimpfen

tune-America. The farmer emerged and stood in the doorway smiling. He had recognized the tune and peered into the light of the coming dawn for the source of the song. Steve approached the farmer smiling.

Wah Lee was an old timer-not old enough to have taken the Long March, but old enough to remember. He welcomed the stranger. By gesture he invited Steve into his one-room cottage and said something to his wife that Steve recognized as friendly words.

Steve sat at the crude table with the farmer and his wife and slowly ate the rice and pork dish set before him. His skill with chopsticks left something to be desired. Communication was difficult too. Steve finally conveyed the idea that he wanted to trade his cap for a conical straw one.Then, indicating his weariness, Steve lay on the pounded dirt floor and slept while his hosts went to the fields.

Day's work done, Wah Lee and his wife shared a simple meal with Steve. Steve stuffed his few belongings in a cloth sack that Wah Lee gave him in exhange for his leather back pack. Some cold rice, a candle stub and towel were Wah Lee's parting gift. They bowed and grinned to each other as Steve expressed his gratitude.

Then he took off in the gathering dusk at six in the evening. China still held to universal time-when it was six pm in Beijing, it was six pm 2800 miles away at the western borders of the land.

The dirt road he followed was easily visible in the moonglow. Steadily the land rose as Steve proceeded west into the foothills of the Daiyun Shan. The people there depended on trade for the rice they needed. They were tin miners and for as far back as memory went they followed the near-vertical veins in the granite rock and drilled and blasted the cassiterite-bearing vein material. They used wheel barrows to tram the ore to the surface where the older men and women and children hammered the ore into small pieces to pick out the black mineral crystals of tin oxide. The gentle slopes would have made deeper levels accessible only by over-long drifts. Hence the skilled miners developed the veins in depth by sinking near vertical internal shafts following the ore down.

With the dawn Steve entered one of the worked out mines and prepared for the day's rest. As the light of the day increased Steve looked from his hideout on the road he had followed to the mine. To his dismay, he saw one of the burley black-clad pursuers.

"How could that have happened?" queried Steve. "I was so damn careful."

He looked again at the man that followed and noted that the man's eyes were frequently on the road. Then it dawned on Steve. He had changed his clothing but held on to the shoes that had left a clear pattern with every step in the dust. He had left an unmistakeable trail that all but a blind man could have followed. And that trail lead directly to Steve's hiding place.

Steve picked up his sack and retreated further into the long unused drift. He felt carefully for any openings in the drift wall and in the floor of the drift in the complete darkness. He moved slowly as he felt ahead with an outstretched leg to seek out any openings. About 200 feet in from the portal, he felt an opening in the floor. Cautiously, he clung to a drift wall as he worked his way around the internal shaft. Just beyond the shaft Steve held his breath and waited.

Soon he heard the cautious movements of his nemesis. Then a loud cry and the noise of the falling body told Steve his pursuer had found the shaft. There were no more sounds. He remembered the candle stub in his sack. He dug it out and lit it. Taking stock of his surroundings by the guttering light of the candle, he looked down the shaft to see the unmoving body of the Chinese at the bottom of the 40 ft.deep steeply inclined shaft.

He backed into a corner of the rectangular shaft and carefully descended. There was no sound but the heavy one of complete silence. There was no pulse on the banged up Chinese. Steve searched the body and took the wad of Chinese money, the man's sandals and a detailed map of southeast China. The candle stub left on the drift shed a dim light. Backing into a corner of the shaft, Steve began his climb to the drift level.

At sixty-seven Steve was still vigorous. It had been many years since he used to scramble up and down mine raises in this manner. Slowly he groped with his hands and feet to find holds on the rough rock walls of the shaft. Every muscle was straining and sweat poured out. Weak with exhaution, he finally made it up to the drift level and laid quiet for a long time to regain his strength.

Now there was one less man trying to catch him. Apparently the group had broken up and took separate ways in seeking him. With luck, he might never even see any of the others. But if he did, at least he was armed and ready.

"I sure don't like the idea of sharing this hole with that Chinaman. I'm gonna' find a better place to hide out for the day. But- wait a minute-there is little chance that another one of that gang is close by. I think I'll make tracks towards the southwest. I've still got about 400 miles to go."

"With my Chinese garments I could pass for a local farmer. If only I could speak the language. I'll have to make out like I'm deaf and dumb. I'll also need to remember that I don't see well enough to read should anyone try to communicate by writing. It's going to be a tough act."

"That map should be of real help. I know I'm in Fujian Province near the Daiyun Shan, at 5,500 feet one of the highest mountain peaks around.

Steve followed the dusty road together with many peasants dressed much as he was. Others walked in the opposite direction. Finally he arrived at the mountain town of Datien where there was a road headed south. His growing beard concealed his skin color and the conical hat did much to conceal his blue eyes. Now and then he was greeted by other travelers and he only nodded briefly in recognition. He would have parted with much of his wad of yuan for a hot meal and a bath. He slept alongside the road for a few more nights before reaching the tin mining town of Zhangping.

Across a river he could see the cloud-shrouded mile high peaks where the tin and tungsten veins were that gave reason for the town's presence. It was tough going without any of the language, so Steve decided he would do a bit of tin mining before moving on. Perhaps he could pick up enough words to ease his passage to Hong Kong A night in a crummy hotel,a simple meal and a bath fortified his aims. The next morning he crossed the river and trudged into the hills to rustle a job.

A surly man stood on the mine dump looking over the morning's crew of job seekers. Steve saw that he asked each job rustler a few questions and then made his decision. No longer was it necessary for everyone to show an identity card or Ho-kou to get a job. Without this registration card one would surely starve

Steve knew what he would do. When the foreman spoke, Steve held out his work-hardened hands and the foreman tapped him on the shoulder. Then Steve followed the other successful applicants as the group headed towards the mine portal. Each man was issued a pick, shovel and a hard hat and they headed underground.

The foreman left Steve at a mine heading where a miner was using a Mexican setup to drill holes in the four-foot wide vein. There was a pile of broken muck on the floor of the

178   Wimpfen

drift. Without hesitation Steve began shoveling the muck into the empty mine car. Then he trammed it towards the portal until he came to a grizzly where he dumped the car. He returned to his heading pushing the empty car ahead of him. That sequence was repeated eight times before they broke for lunch.

Both Steve and the miner walked to the grizzly and sat on a bench to eat the bowl of rice and fish provided by the company. It was a meager meal but assured the company that it's workers had enough to eat to do their job. This was the system in activities such as mining that were government operated under the Peoples Communist Party.

The miner mumbled, "My name is T'ao Chu *Nin gui xing?*"

Steve guessed at the question and replied "Ess Teev." The young miner looked up as he passed a chunk of ore from hand to hand. He tossed it to Steve with the single word "Catch." Steve looked up, caught the rock and looked at the laughing miner.

"Gotcha'" said the miner and Steve grinned.

"How did you know I spoke English.?"

"I not sure, but blue eyes not Chinese,so I try. No worry, I not tell."

"How come you speak English?"

"My father, he have television. So I learn."

"Where do you live?"

"I live with mother, father and young sister in Zhangping. Father one time he miner. I geologist University of Tientsin.."

"Why do you work as a miner when you're trained as a geologist?"

"No jobs as geologist. Local cell of Peoples Communist Party assign me work in tin mines."

Steve was thrilled at seeing each day the fresh face of ore. It reminded him of those long-ago days when he was busy mining those precious gold quartz specimens. Here he took great pleasure in seeing the black crystals of cassiterite revealed in each new face often associated with crystals of wolframite. He collected some and took them when he returned to the dormitory that was his home at the mining camp. There he shared a long room with nineteen other men. They slept on pallets on the rammed earth floor.

He looked forward each day to working with T'ao Chu who enlarged his small vocabulary of Han. T'ao Chu also told him much about China.

"China great land! Many peoples! In 4,000 year China has 500 million peoples. In thirty more years, China peoples one billion. Food increase but no enough. Too many peoples! China only small amount bigger than USA. We have 3.7 million square miles. You are 3.6 million. But much land China not good for grow food. Tibetan plateau at 10,000 ft. up and Taklamakan desert Xinjiang no good for nothing! Only one-tenth China good for grow food-only quarter acre per person. We Chinese close to starve ally time."

"There may be solution to this problem. Smaller people and lower sperm count could result in less impact on limited food supplies." Steve elaborated on this concept as T'ao Chu consistently nodded his head in agreement.

"Just what China need! Smaller-fewer and eveybody live better. Why that Kut Hing try stop?"

"That's hard to understand but I think they want China to rule world by having bigger people."

"You must come visit my home Zhangping. Tell my father your ideas."

Steve agreed as he was interested in visiting a Chinese home. They planned to go down to the town for the next rest period. Work was continuous for fifteen days, then there was a five day rest before the cycle began again.

Walking down to the village they admired the misty peaks and watched the sun dispel the soft clouds as the day advanced. In the village they sought out T'ao Chu's home, a single room mud-walled house with a tiny garden. Inside, what little furniture they had was immovable. The bed, the table and the several chairs were built of dried mud that had been shaped to serve it's purpose. A single small bulb was the only illumination and an extension cord went to the treasured TV that was their window on the rest of the world.

Father Chu was a slender and bent man about 5 ft 8 in. tall. He smiled at Steve as his wrinkled face shone in welcome of their foreign guest. Mother Chu stayed in the background as she bustled around preparing the rice that would be their next meal.

Steve asked T'ao why they lived like this. "This home is so different from what the world is told about China."

"I know! Communist party wish convey idea China strong and rich, but not so. My mother and father live better off than most. Papa is educated man-teacher. Not have much but *Ma-mu-le*, we survive. I not happy look forward to this life. I want go your land and learn better ways, then return here and help others."

"Do you really want to leave your homeland?"

"I do want leave. Not for me is to stay in rut. If I stay China then my life leave mark like stick finger in pail of water and pull it out."

"You have choice. When I leave here I'll return to my homeland. You can come with me if authorities in some US Embassy agree."

"I like go America with you. But how you go?"

"I thought I might go to Hong Kong and fly home from there."

"Not good idea. In Hong Kong you stick head in lion's mouth. Kut Hing and those bad men's headquarter there and all looking for you. Must have better way. But first must make you look more Chinese. We go eye doctor and get you black contacts. Dye hair. You speak enough Chinese dialect, but must change look. Me travel as your son and we go by Xiamen."

"That sounds like a good idea to me. What's more, Hong Kong far away and Xiamen is near."

"From Zhangping easy to get to Xiamen. Every few days train take tin concentrate to smelter Xiamen. We ride on car of tin concentrates. Nobody care."

When the next five-day rest period came, T'ao Chu took Steve to an optician in Zhangping. There he was fitted with contact lenses that made him appear to have eyes as dark as those of T'ao Chu.

It was easy to board the train. The cars were loaded with tin concentrates a car at a time. Steve and T'ao Chu took some old sacks on which to sit and climbed aboard a loaded car. The load of tin concentrates settled into a peak and left open corners where they could sit and still not be seen from the track level. It was a bumpy, jostling ride but six hours later the train pulled into a smelter yard in Xiamen. In the gathering dusk, they left the train and sought a small hotel where they washed well to rid them of the black dust of the tin concentrates. They needed a nights rest before looking for a way to get to Quemoy in the NRC.

"What we do for money? This all I got." said T'ao Chu waving fifteen bills in the air.

"Don't worry. When I climbed down to make sure that guy was dead, I took his money and his wad of bills amounts to 20,000 Yuan. It's all in 10 Yuan notes."

"That 10 Yuan note biggest bill PRC make."

" I think we should go to Taipei. They know me at the hotel where I stayed and I know the U.S. Ambassador. We should be able to get some help from him. But first we go to Quemoy. From Quemoy we can fly to Taipei."

They wandered around the waterfront looking at launches and talking with some of the skippers. Finally they found one amenable to risk crossing the narrow strait between the PRC and the NRC island of Quemoy. It took 5,000 Yuan to firm up the skipper's resolve to make the forbidden crossing.

Three nights later they left at midnight for the short trip to Quemoy. The launch touched land on an isolated beach, put the two passengers ashore and left.

A few hours later Steve and T'ao Chu reached the airport. At a giveaway rate of exchange Steve got rid of all the PRC yuan in exchange for two seats on the daily flight to Taipei.

"Hi Nina, it's me."

"Steve! What happened to you? We had just about given up on ever seeing you again. It's been three months since your last call!"

"I understand, honey! It's been a rough go and I'll tell you all about it when I get home. Right now all I can think of is to be there and have you in my arms. I'm well but kind of hungry. Food is hard to come by in China. Send me some money. I'll get out of these Chinese duds and get home pronto. I've got a young man I hope to bring home, so you'd better send me about three or four thousand bucks care of the Embassy."

"OK. Will do, but hurry I need you and am so damn glad you'll be home soon. I can hardly wait! It's so good to hear your voice. Love you-hurry, hurry! Bye."

A call to the Embassy resulted in transportation to the city. The money was waiting for him. A flight the next day would take them to San Francisco and on to Denver. The US Ambassador issued a tourist entry permit to T'ao Chu. Later on some arrangements would be needed to permit him a longer stay in the US.

On the long trans-Pacific flight, Steve organized his thoughts. He looked forward to telling his family and the Musters of his experiences during his long absence. He chatted with T'ao Chung who was nervously eager to see the United States and to improve his English.

"What a lot has happened to this world in these past forty years." thought Steve. "There are still a lot of us big people around, but the numbers of "smaller" folk are increasing. Birth rates are declining. Our team has been notably successful in achieving the goal of smaller-fewer. But what about greed? Would there ever be a way to reduce that trait in human kind? It was a worthy goal. But it would have to be left to another generation."

He was tired.

- 30 -